Night of the Armada

D. P. Conway

Dear Ireland
Series

Book 1

Day Lights Publishing House, Inc.
Cleveland, Ohio

Darkness to Light through the Power of Story

DEAR IRELAND
BY D.P. CONWAY
DEAR IRELAND
AT THE CROSSROADS
THE MEMOIR OF BRIDGIE NED CAMPBELL CONWAY OF DOONA, BALLYCROY
D.P. CONWAY
DEAR IRELAND
NIGHT OF THE ARMADA
D.P. CONWAY
DEAR IRELAND
BRIDGIE NED AND THE CASE OF THE MISSING PIG
D.P. CONWAY
DEAR IRELAND
ROSE OF DOONA
D.P. CONWAY
DEAR IRELAND
MARY MAC
D.P. CONWAY
DEAR IRELAND
OH, DANNY BOY
D.P. CONWAY

Dedications

For Marisa
We have deeply shared life's journey.
Cara Femmina, Solo Tu
Io Ti Amo Sempre

For my Children
Thank you for Encouraging Me

For Aubrey, Avery, and Charlie
May you be Inspired by this Story

For Sonny and Mary Conway,
and their Children, Danny, Teresa, Tony, and John,
Whose life in Ireland made this Book Possible

Shipwreck

The Santa Maria Encoronada
Off the Coast of Western Ireland, September 21, 1588

"Captain! Land ahead!"

Don Alonso's breath hitched, his heart pounding as his eyes snapped open. Rain blurred his vision, but through the storm's violent whip, he saw it—a jagged sliver of land rising like the maw of a terrible beast. Too close. Far too close. Panic flickered at the edge of his mind, a feeling he hadn't indulged in years.

"Rudder hard right! Rudder hard right!" he bellowed, forcing the command out through gritted teeth. The wind snatched his words, twisting them into the storm's howling fury. His soaked coat hung heavy, suffocating him as if the storm itself sought to drag him under. Shielding his eyes from the stinging rain, Alonso fought to suppress the fear tightening like a vice around his chest.

The ship lurched violently, plunging into the roiling black sea. A massive wave crashed over the bow, slamming into Alonso like an icy wall. The impact stole his breath and sent him sprawling against the ship's side. Pain exploded through his ribs, but it was the creeping dread that clung to him. He clawed desperately at the slick wood, lungs burning from saltwater.

We're going to die.

Alonso shoved the thought aside and forced himself to his feet. Each step was a battle against the storm and his rising fear. He couldn't afford to falter. Staggering back to the wheel, he joined the trembling helmsman, their hands gripping the wood as they fought to steer the ship through the storm's fury.

"Keep turning!" Alonso's voice was hoarse, nearly lost to the storm's roar. Ahead loomed two jagged peaks rising like sentinels from the sea. Unforgiving. Inescapable. The nearest peak stretched toward them, as if the mountain itself sought to swallow them whole. The ship's turn was agonizingly slow, its groans lost in the storm's rage. They might avoid the first peak, but the second jutted out like a predator's claw.

Four days. Four cursed days of this relentless storm. Alonso had weathered tempests before, but this storm felt alive, malevolent. Ireland was different. The cold seeped into his bones, freezing him from the inside. He shouldn't have come here. Death lurked just beyond the waves, its gaze fixed on them.

God help us.

For the first time in years, Alonso thought of his wife waiting on the shore in Spain, her face lined with worry as she scanned the horizon for a ship that might never return. His daughters would never know why their father never came back.

His eyes darted to the port side. There! A bay lay in the distance, offering a slim chance at salvation. Could they turn in time? Could they reach it?

"Turn port side! Rudder port side!" he ordered, but his voice lacked its usual strength. Control was slipping, the ship lurching wildly beneath his feet.

"Lower the sails!" Alonso barked, his voice raw with desperation. The order felt futile against the storm's fury, but it was their only hope. He saw hesitation in the crew.

"Now!" Alonso shouted again, urgency cracking his voice. Control was slipping through his fingers. Then the air split with a thunderous crack—the mast snapped in two, crashing down with a sickening roar. It swung out toward the starboard side, dragging rigging with it, before smashing into the deck. Men screamed as the ship buckled, its side splitting open like a wound.

Alonso's stomach churned. It was over.

"Heave! Ho! Heave! Ho!" the crew shouted, their voices trembling as they rushed to lift the broken mast. Two men lay crushed beneath its weight, their bodies twisted grotesquely. One still gasped for breath, mumbling incoherent prayers. The other was already gone.

"Get them below!" Alonso's voice was hoarse, barely audible above the storm. His hands shook as he clenched his fists, willing himself to keep moving, to keep fighting.

The great ship surged up and down, careening through the waves like a beast in its death throes. The broken mast hung precariously, threatening to plunge them into the sea at any moment. Alonso considered ordering it cut away. What if it was their only chance? What if it helped them survive?

The storm howled, dragging them closer to the jagged coast of Ireland. Don Alonso, soaked and battered, clung to the railing, his body shaking with exhaustion, his mind swirling with fear and regret. For the first time in years, he prayed.

But even as the words formed on his lips, he knew—prayers wouldn't save them.

Santa Maria Encoronada

The Storm

Black Sod Bay, Western of Ireland
September 21, 1588

Nora McManamon sighed, wiping sweat from her brow. She knelt before the sputtering fire, her bare knees pressing into the cold, damp earth. Everything felt wet—soaked through by the storm that had battered their home and lives for four long, terrible days. Her fingers trembled as she tried to coax warmth from the embers. But it wasn't just the cold that gnawed at her. It was the rising panic she'd felt for days which she refused to let show.

She turned to her youngest, now awake. "Go out behind the house and get another bucket of turf, Peggy," Nora's voice was sharper than she intended. She winced inwardly, regretting the edge in her tone. The relentless storm had frayed her nerves. Where was Daniel and Ronan?

Hold it together. You have to.

"Peggy, wear yer blanket and go fast," she called again, softening her voice this time, a wave of guilt washing over her. She hadn't meant to be harsh. But how much more could they endure? How long before everything crumbled?

"Yes, Ma," Peggy's voice was barely audible, as if she didn't want to be noticed. Nora glanced at her daughter, watching the girl wrap a thin, threadbare blanket around her small shoulders. So young, Nora thought, yet there was something in Peggy's eyes that hadn't been there before—a shadow of understanding. The storm had shaken them all, but Peggy was starting to see things, to understand the fragility of their lives in a way Nora wished she didn't.

Her husband and youngest son still hadn't returned. They had gone out to check on her eldest son Patrick's family a half hour ago, and there had been no word. Sure it was only a quarter mile down the cow path trail, but in this storm… was there something wrong? The unspoken fear hung heavy and oppressive.

Peggy moved toward the door, her small frame bracing for the cold as she opened it, stepped into the storm, and closed the door behind her.

Nora's heart clenched. She bit her lip, hands tightening around the rag she used to stoke the fire. She should've gone herself. Peggy was still so young. But she could not let the fire go out. And her eldest, Catherine, was asleep, exhausted from the long day of caring for her bedridden sister, Marie. Nora took a deep breath, telling herself that Peggy would be fine. The storm might frighten her a bit, but it would only be a minute or two. Was it right to send a child into that chaos? There was no choice now—only survival.

~ ~ ~ ~

Outside, Peggy's heart raced as the storm's icy wind lashed against her, the bucket she carried nearly ripped from her hands. Every step was a struggle, her legs trembling as she fought to stay upright. She could barely see, the rain stinging her face like needles. Her hands ached from the cold, fingers clutching the bucket tightly as the wind tried to pull her away. It was stronger than her, and for a terrifying moment, she thought the storm might win.

Where are Da and Ronan?

The thought gnawed at her, cutting deeper than the cold. Her dad Daniel and her brother Ronan had only gone to her brother Patrick's house—a quarter-mile down the cow trail. They'd said they would be right back. They'd promised. But promises didn't mean much when the world was breaking apart.

As Peggy reached the turf pile, her body trembling, she felt something shift—a strange heaviness in the air, as if the storm had paused for just a moment.

Her heart skipped.

She froze, her eyes drawn out to the sea, compelled by a force she didn't understand. There—on the horizon—a dark shape loomed in the distance, bobbing violently on the waves. Her breath caught. At first, she thought she was imagining it.

No...

But it was real.

A ship—massive, wild, and thrashing against the storm—was coming straight for the shore. It was coming for them.

For a moment, Peggy couldn't breathe. Her body locked in place, her mind racing. It didn't feel real. It felt like a nightmare she couldn't wake from.

Then, as if the fear snapped her into action, she dropped the bucket and ran for the house, her heart pounding so hard it threatened to burst.

"Ma! Ma!" she screamed, her voice thin and trembling, fighting against the storm's roar. Panic gripped her—real, bone-deep fear. It wasn't just the storm anymore. It was something bigger. Something worse.

Nora turned, her eyes widening as Peggy's screams pierced the cabin. "What is it, Peggy? What happened?"

"There's a ship!" Peggy's voice cracked, the words tumbling out in a rush. "A massive ship, bigger than our house! It's comin' right for us!"

Nora's stomach twisted into knots. She rushed to the door, shoving it open with all her strength, the wind nearly tearing it from her hands.

Her breath caught in her throat as she stared out at the bay, waves crashing furiously into the fields no more than 500 feet away.

There it was.

A monstrous ship, tossed mercilessly by the storm, its masts broken and its sails torn to shreds. It was being driven toward them—straight toward the shore—by waves so large they seemed like mountains.

"Holy Mother of God," Nora whispered, her voice barely audible, trembling with dread. She had never seen anything like it. The ship was enormous, reeling and swaying, barely clinging to life. It was doomed. And so were they.

"They're going to crash," Peggy said, her voice a small, terrified whisper.

"Get inside!" Nora shouted, pushing Peggy back toward the fire, her hands shaking. She turned to the bed where her other daughters lay. "Catherine! Get up, now!"

"What is it, Ma?" Catherine mumbled, still not fully awake.

Nora's voice rose with desperation. "There's a ship comin' in! It's going to crash! You need to go to Patrick's house and tell yer Da to come home! And tell Ronan to run to the castle—and warn them!"

Catherine stared at her wide-eyed, the fear slowly sinking in. She threw off her blanket, grabbing the nearest wrap for warmth.

"I'll go with her!" Peggy exclaimed, her voice tight.

"No, Peggy. I need you here."

Nora shoved Catherine toward the door, her pulse pounding in her ears. "Warn the neighbors on the way. Go, now!"

Catherine didn't hesitate. She ran into the storm, disappearing into the wind and rain.

For a moment, Nora stood frozen, her heart in her throat. The ship was closer now, so close it felt like it might crash into their fields at any second. Where was Daniel? I need to tell Farrell.

She turned to Peggy. "Stay here with Marie. I need to warn yer Uncle Farrell." Her voice wavered, but she forced herself to sound calm. "I'll be right back. I promise."

Peggy Sees the Ship from Shore

At Patrick's House

Catherine burst through the door, gasping for breath, her legs aching from the cold. Inside, her father Daniel and brothers Patrick and Ronan sat around the table, while Patrick's wife and child huddled by the fire. The warmth inside was a stark contrast to the chaos outside.

"What are ye doin' here, Catherine?" Daniel's voice was sharp with surprise as he saw the panic in her eyes.

"There's a ship!" Catherine panted, her voice hoarse. "Ma says it's comin' right for the shore! She sent me to tell ye to come home, and Ronan needs to run to the castle to warn them!"

Daniel shot to his feet, his face paling. Swinging the door open, he stepped outside and froze.

There it was. A massive, dark ship, barely holding together against the crashing waves. Too close. A shadow of death hurtling toward the rocks.

"Oh, no," Daniel muttered. He turned sharply to his sons. "Ronan, go to the castle," he ordered. Ronan was already moving. "Patrick, stay with yer family. Catherine, come with me."

Patrick nodded, wide-eyed. Catherine swallowed hard and followed her father back into the storm, the cold biting deep as soon as they stepped outside.

"Go, Ronan! Hurry!" Daniel barked. There was no time to think—only action.

Ronan was seventeen, tall and lanky, his sandy brown hair tousled by the winds. His piercing blue eyes, freckled skin, and broadening shoulders hinted at a youth hardened by the harsh coastal life. He moved with a quiet determination, his jaw set against the storm. Though still young, there was a weight in his gaze—a boy growing into a man, carrying the resolve of someone who had already faced life's harsh realities. Without hesitation, he sprinted toward the castle, the storm roaring around him.

Ronan

Uncle Farrell

Nora McManamon pounded on the door of the house closer to the shore, her fist slamming against the wood as the wind howled around her. "Farrell! Farrell!" Her voice was swallowed by the storm, but she kept banging, her heart racing. Terror gripped her.

Finally, the door swung open. Farrell filled the doorway, his massive frame unmoving against the storm's fury. His face was stern, carved by years of salt air and worry, but something in his sharp brown eyes flickered—something calculating and dangerous.

"Nora, why are ye poundin' on me door? What's wrong?" His voice boomed over the storm, rough and impatient.

"Farrell, ye need to see this!" Nora gasped, grabbing his arm and pulling him outside. The wind slammed into them, nearly knocking her off her feet. Farrell stood steady as a rock but froze when he followed her frantic pointing.

A monstrous black ship loomed against the sea, barely holding together as the storm drove it mercilessly toward the rocks.

"Mother of God," Farrell muttered, his jaw tightening, fists clenching. The fury of the storm didn't faze him, but his eyes stayed fixed on the doomed vessel.

"What do we do?" Nora's voice cracked, trembling with fear.

Farrell's eyes didn't leave the ship. "I'm goin' down to the shore. Tell Daniel to meet me there."

Nora's heart stuttered. "By yerself? Farrell, ye can't—" She stopped. Arguing with Farrell was useless. He always did what he set his mind to. But the thought of him alone, facing the wreck and whatever it brought, chilled her to the bone.

"There's no one else to do it, is there?" he said sharply, cutting through the wind like a blade. "I'll deal with whatever comes." His massive shoulders hunched against the storm as he turned toward the shore.

Nora stood frozen, watching him stride into the field, fear and dread swirling in her chest. She wanted to stop him, but the words wouldn't come. Then she remembered and shouted, "Ronan's gone to warn the castle!" But Farrell didn't hear her. He was already too far.

Turning back, Nora ran home, her feet slipping in the mud as her heart pounded. As she glanced over her shoulder, she saw Farrell disappearing toward the shore, the storm seeming to part around him. He looked invincible, but for the first time, she wondered if even Farrell could withstand what was coming.

Farrell McManamon

At Grace's Castle

Ronan's legs burned as he neared Grace O'Malley's castle, the wind howling with fury. His breath came in ragged gasps, each step a battle against the storm. The castle loomed ahead, its stone walls dark against the stormy sky. He slammed his fist against the heavy wooden door.

"Open up!" Ronan shouted, his voice nearly lost in the storm. For a moment, he feared no one had heard, but then the door creaked open. One of Grace O'Malley's soldiers appeared, his face hard and suspicious.

"What is it?" the man barked.

"There's a ship," Ronan gasped, pointing toward the sea. "It's about to crash on the shore!"

The soldier's eyes widened. Without a word, he turned, shouting, "Get up! Move now!" Soldiers poured out of the castle—twenty men, grim-faced and armed. These were battle-hardened men, ready for the storm's chaos. Ian Flynn, their wiry leader, emerged, his sharp blue eyes cutting through the rain.

Flynn grabbed Ronan's arm roughly. "Where?" he demanded.

Ronan pointed to the sea. Through the rain, the ship's tattered sails with red crosses were visible. Flynn's face hardened.

"We've no time," Flynn growled. "Move!"

Ronan ran ahead, soldiers close behind, their boots sinking into the soaked ground. The wind bit into their faces, and the roar of the sea grew louder. When they reached the shore, the sight was worse than Ronan had imagined. The massive ship was nearly on the rocks.

"They won't make it," one soldier muttered.

Flynn drew his sword. "Stay sharp. If there are survivors, they could be trouble."

Ronan's stomach churned. Survivors? Pirates? Soldiers? He shoved the fear aside, focusing on the wreck. Flynn barked orders to two soldiers. "Lynch! O'Connor! Ride to Rockfleet. Now."

"But the storm—" Lynch started.

"The storm's the least of yer worries. If ye're not fast enough, Grace O'Malley will have yer hides. Go!"

The men cursed but mounted their horses, galloping into the night. Flynn turned back to the sea as the ship lurched against the rocks.

"We'll save who we can," Flynn muttered, "but Grace will want answers. And if we don't have them, we're damned."

Ronan stood frozen, the weight of Flynn's words sinking in. Even in her absence, Grace O'Malley's presence loomed. Flynn's sharp voice jolted him. "Stay ready. This is just the beginning."

Ronan nodded, fear twisting in his gut as the storm screamed and the waves crashed, carrying the promise of something far worse.

Castle of Grace O'Malley, the Pirate Queen

Ian Flynn, In Charge of the Castle

In the Fields

Farrell's boots sank into the soaked ground, each step slow and deliberate as he moved toward the shore. The wind whipped at his face, stinging his skin, but he didn't blink. His eyes were locked on the ship—a looming shadow teetering on the edge of disaster. He had seen storms before, but this was different. There was a weight in the air, a darkness that gnawed at him.

As the great ship lurched closer, every wave dragging it nearer to the jagged rocks spread along the strand, Farrell's muscles tensed. He felt the storm's raw power, the inevitable clash. He didn't run—he never did. There was no stopping what was about to happen. His mind was racing, calculating every possibility. Who was aboard? Were they friend or foe? Whatever came off that ship would spill onto his shore, his land. And Farrell wasn't the kind of man to let that go unanswered.

His jaw clenched. Daniel needed to get here soon. Farrell wasn't afraid of a fight, but something about this night felt different. Darker. The storm wasn't just trying to break the ship—it was trying to throw something dangerous onto the land.

Farrell glanced back toward the village, toward the place where Nora had run. She and the children would be safe, wouldn't they? But what if they weren't? If the ship's crew came ashore desperate, half-mad from the storm, what would they do?

The ship groaned a terrible, creaking sound that sent a shiver down Farrell's spine. It was close now, so close. Farrell flexed his fingers, the muscles in his arms tightening. He was ready for a fight if it came to that. But deep down, he felt a flicker of doubt, a small voice whispering that this was bigger than him. Bigger than all of them.

~ ~ ~ ~

The wind tore at Peggy's shawl, whipping it around her as she clung to her father's side. Daniel McManamon stood silent, his eyes fixed on the distant shape of the ship, broken and barely afloat. Around them, the people of Doona gathered on the embankment, keeping safe from the waves but close enough to witness the wreck. Nearby, Grace O'Malley's soldiers stood ready, their faces a mix of anticipation and wariness.

Flynn, one of Grace's trusted men, appeared beside them, his face hardened as his sharp gaze swept over the beach.

"Who are they?" Daniel asked, his voice low, his eyes never leaving the ship.

"The Spanish," Flynn said simply, tension threading his tone.

Peggy's heart lurched. She didn't fully understand, but she'd heard the whispers about the Spanish Armada. The enemy, it seemed, had arrived.

Daniel's jaw tightened. "What'll we do with them?"

Flynn's eyes flicked from the ship to Daniel. "We'll save who we can. That's what the Dark Lady would want." His voice was steady, but the weight of his words silenced the crowd. "But stay on guard. They're soldiers, and if they turn on us…" He let the warning hang heavy in the air.

Peggy's heart raced as she glanced between Flynn and her father. She knew Grace O'Malley's reputation—a leader both fierce and merciful, loyal to her people above all. The Spanish, though battered and broken by the storm, remained a threat.

The Crash

The wind shrieked as Ronan and Patrick appeared on the embankment, sprinting through the rain-soaked grass to join their father, Daniel. Their eyes locked on the sea, where the Spanish ship fought a losing battle against the waves. Peggy clutched her father's coat, her wide eyes fixed on the battered ship.

The ship rose on a monstrous wave, tilting skyward in a desperate plea for mercy. For a moment, it hung suspended against the darkened sky. Then, with a deafening crack, it smashed against the jagged rocks. The earth seemed to shake beneath them as the sound echoed across the shore.

"There it goes!" someone shouted, and the beach erupted in chaos. Shouts filled the air as men pointed toward the wreck, their voices rising above the storm.

Bodies were flung into the churning waves, the sea tearing at the ship with relentless fury. Peggy's breath caught as she saw men scrambling on the deck, clinging to the rails, others slipping beneath the waves. One man flailed as he was thrown overboard, swallowed whole by the sea. A gasp escaped her lips.

The ship spun sideways under the force of another wave, its main mast snapping with a crack, toppling into the water as it rolled onto its side. Flynn's voice rang out, cutting through the chaos. "Move! Get the sailors out of the water!"

Daniel turned to Peggy, urgency etched into his face. "Stay here, Peggy. Stay safe." He squeezed her shoulder before racing toward the shore with the other men. Flynn's commanding voice echoed over the storm. "Right, then! Move, all of ye! Those men won't survive long. Doona's brave—show it now!"

The men of Doona surged forward, soldiers from the castle among them, their faces grim and determined. They braved the wind and rain, pulling half-drowned sailors to safety. Peggy stood frozen, her heart pounding as her father and brothers hauled men from the waves, their muscles straining with effort.

"Come on! Swim!" Peggy whispered, her voice lost in the storm. She didn't know these men, but their fight against the sea pulled at her heart. She willed them to survive.

Her gaze darted to a man thrown into the water, his arms reaching before the sea closed over him. Peggy's heart clenched as she whispered, "Please, make it." He didn't resurface, and tears blurred her vision. The storm's fury blinded her, but she couldn't look away. The people of Doona defied the sea, dragging survivors to shore against impossible odds.

"Peggy, are ye all right?" Her mother, Nora, and her sister, Catherine, appeared beside her, breathless. "I'm all right, Ma," Peggy yelled back, her voice trembling. She pointed toward the shore. "Look at Uncle Farrell."

Farrell ran like a man possessed, leaping into the waves with no hesitation. He hauled a man from the water as though he weighed nothing, his face grim but unyielding. Peggy watched, wide-eyed, as her father, brothers, and Farrell worked alongside the villagers and soldiers to save the sailors. The sea fought to claim them, but the men of Doona fought harder.

A scream pierced the air. Peggy's gaze snapped to a man pinned beneath part of the ship's mast, his leg trapped, his face twisted in agony. The mast shifted with a wave, and he broke free, his leg trailing blood as he was carried toward shore. Peggy watched, breathless. He flailed, his arms weakly fighting the waves. Her heart clenched as she willed him to make it.

The man reached the sand and collapsed. Peggy stood frozen, her eyes fixed on him. He hadn't moved. Was he alive? She didn't know, and the uncertainty gripped her heart like a vice.

Sailors Struggling to Shore. The Doona Villagers try to Help.

Ronan Rescues Don Alonso

Ronan spotted him first—a man slipping beneath the surface, the water swallowing him whole. He didn't think. He ran.

His focus locked on the figure floundering in the waves, arms thrashing, head barely visible. The storm was relentless, the sea a wild beast, but Ronan pushed forward, his heart pounding as he sprinted across the embankment. Without hesitation, he plunged into the surf. Each wave struck like a battering ram, cold and hard, but he fought through, high-stepping against the crashing water. With a final dive, he disappeared beneath the waves.

"Ronan!" Daniel's voice pierced the storm, sharp with panic.

"Da, where is he?" Peggy's voice trembled, her wide eyes scanning the sea.

"There!" she screamed, pointing frantically.

Ronan surfaced, thrashing through the waves, arms reaching for the struggling man. The sailor, weak and desperate, grabbed at him, dragging him under. Panic flared in Ronan's chest as water rushed into his lungs. For a moment, chaos consumed him—the sea's grip, the man's weight, the pull of the current. But Ronan fought back. With a swift punch, he knocked the man unconscious, stopping the struggle. Hooking an arm around the sailor's neck, Ronan began the grueling swim back to shore.

Every stroke was a battle. The waves crashed over them, pulling them under again and again. Ronan's muscles screamed, his lungs burned, but he kept going, dragging the man inch by inch through the water. When he finally reached the shore, his legs gave out, collapsing onto the sand. Beside him, the sailor lay limp, pale and still.

Daniel was there in seconds, his voice a mix of anger and relief. "Ronan, ye mad fool. Are ye all right?"

Ronan nodded, wiping salt water from his face, gasping for air. "Aye, Da, I'm fine."

Daniel exhaled, his face softening briefly before urgency returned. The strand was chaotic—debris and survivors scattered in the gray light of dawn. The tide was retreating, the storm's fury easing. "I'll be back," Daniel said, heading to help others.

Ronan stood, legs shaking, scanning the scene. His father and the men worked tirelessly, pulling sailors from the waves, while the women of Doona brought blankets and provisions. The sailor he'd saved stirred, his eyes fluttering open, blinking against the dim light. His lips moved, but no sound came at first.

Ronan knelt beside him. The man's voice, weak and hoarse, broke the silence. "Who… who are you?" His accent was unmistakably Spanish.

"Ronan," he replied, offering a small smile. "Ye were goin' under. I pulled ye out."

The man's eyes flickered with realization, gratitude softening his expression. "You… saved me."

"Aye, I did." Ronan nodded.

Before the sailor could speak again, another voice cut through the air, sharp with urgency. "Captain! Captain!"

Ronan turned to see another sailor running toward them, panic in his eyes. He knelt beside the man Ronan had saved, helping him sit up. Ronan stepped back as the two exchanged rapid words in Spanish, their voices too quiet to catch.

The captain, now more alert, turned to Ronan, his gaze steady and filled with gratitude. He grasped Ronan's hands firmly. "Thank you," he said, his voice hoarse but strong. "I owe you my life."

Ronan blinked, caught off guard by the intensity of the man's words. "What's yer name?" he asked quietly.

The man straightened, his posture proud despite his battered state. "I am Captain Don Alonso. I am in your debt."

Ronan nodded. "Happy to have helped ye."

Don Alonso returned the nod, his exhaustion evident but his steps determined as he moved toward his scattered crew. Ronan watched him go, a strange sense of pride and relief washing over him. He had saved a life, and amidst the storm's chaos, that felt like the only victory that mattered.

Ronan Saves Captain Don Alonso

Daniel and Flynn

Daniel wiped the rain from his eyes, his gaze fixed on the half-dead sailors lying scattered across the sand. Every instinct in him screamed to pull them to shelter, to get them out of the storm before the cold claimed them.

"We need to get the injured into the houses," Daniel shouted to Flynn, desperation cutting through his voice. "They won't last much longer out here."

Flynn turned to him, his face hard, eyes flashing with warning. "No," he said firmly, his voice low but resolute. "Leave them where they are. They're the Spanish, Daniel. They've brought the possibility of England's wrath upon our shores with them. We don't know what danger they might bring if we let them inside."

Daniel's jaw clenched. He glanced back at the sailors, battered and broken, barely clinging to life. His heart twisted with compassion, but Flynn's words hammered at him, unyielding.

"Grace O'Malley was supposed to be here days ago," Flynn continued, his tone as sharp as a blade. "The Dark Lady of Doona won't look kindly on us showing mercy to the enemy without her say in it. She'll expect us to be cautious, to act with loyalty—not sentiment."

Daniel felt a wave of frustration and helplessness rise within him. The image of Grace, fierce and unyielding, lingered in his mind. He knew the strength of her wrath and the expectations she held over the people. Defying Flynn now, when her arrival was imminent, would mean risking more than just his own safety.

He took one last look at the sailors, the bitter taste of resignation filling his mouth.

Finally, he dropped his gaze and nodded stiffly, the weight of the decision pressing down on him. "Fine," he muttered, his voice barely audible above the storm. "We'll wait until she returns."

The words tasted bitter, but he knew he had little choice. With one final, reluctant glance at the suffering men on the shore, Daniel turned back to the others, guiding them to continue pulling the sailors clear of the water without taking them too close to the village.

Peggy Finds Rodrigo

Peggy could wait no longer. She sprinted down the shoreline, her feet slipping in the wet sand as the wind pushed against her. Her breath was ragged, her heart pounding. She had seen him—a man who had crawled ashore, barely alive. He couldn't be left to die.

"Peggy, wait!" Nora's voice rang out behind her, sharp with urgency, but Peggy didn't slow. "Over here, Ma!" she shouted, her voice cracking. "There's one over here!"

She dropped to her knees beside the man, her trembling hands touching his cold, pale face. "Wake up! Wake up!" she pleaded, shaking him gently, her small frame shaking as panic rose in her chest.

Nora reached her, breathless and wide-eyed at the man's condition. "Oh, Peggy…" she murmured, fear lacing her voice. Kneeling, she moved to the man's legs and gasped at the jagged splinter of wood lodged deep in his thigh, blood pooling beneath him. She pressed two fingers to his nose, holding her breath. Relief washed over her. "He's breathing," she exhaled, though faintly.

Her gaze shot toward their house, just 300 feet away but feeling miles distant. She stood abruptly, shouting, "Daniel! Come here!"

Daniel turned at her cry, his face hardening. Without hesitation, he motioned to Patrick, and they ran toward her, their boots kicking up wet sand. Both men stopped short at the sight of the sailor's injury. Patrick paled at the wood jutting from the man's thigh.

"We have to get him into the house," Nora said firmly, though fear edged her tone. "And we have to remove that splinter."

Daniel nodded. "Aye. We'll need more hands." Turning, he called out, "Ronan! Farrell!"

Ronan, weary from rescuing sailors, wiped his brow and ran toward them. Farrell followed, slower but steady, his face grim. "We'll have to carry him," Daniel said, bending over the man. "Careful with his leg."

"What about Flynn?" Ronan asked nervously, glancing down the strand toward the castle.

Daniel's jaw tightened. "Flynn's not here. It's our duty."

Farrell's voice was low. "He's one of the Spanish. Flynn won't like it."

Daniel's eyes narrowed. "Flynn's not the leader of me. Grace O'Malley's man or not, we save lives here. Now, help me lift him."

Farrell hesitated, then nodded. The four bent down, carefully lifting the sailor, avoiding the splinter in his leg. The man groaned, his head lolling as they carried him. Step by step, through the lashing storm and wet sand, they made their way toward the house, every movement deliberate and heavy with urgency.

Marie Listens

The wind rattled the old stone walls of the McManamon house as Marie sat by the small hearth, wrapped in a woolen shawl. Her pale fingers traced the beads of her rosary, though her mind was far from prayer. The weak fire crackled, casting shadows across the room, but the chill lingered, deep within her bones, unmoved by blankets or wool.

Whatever was happening outside, she couldn't be part of it. She was too sick, and the storm's chill could kill her. A sharp cough tore through her chest, her hand rising instinctively to her throat. Over the last six months, the illness had rooted itself in her, an unwelcome guest whispering her limitations. She was now the fragile sister, the one who would never marry, never travel, never live the life of other village women.

Her fingers stilled on the rosary, her eyes drifting to the window where the faint outline of the fields beyond was visible. For a moment, the wind had died down. The cough returned, harsh and insistent, a cruel reminder of her place in the world. Her life seemed destined for the quiet of the hearth and the confinement of four walls. Marriage was a faded dream, slipping further from her reach.

Yet, as her grip tightened on the rosary, a small voice inside dared to whisper, *What if?* What if her life held more than this frailty? What if Heaven had other plans?

Men's shouts outside broke her reverie. She couldn't remain idle. Rising, she ran outside into the teeming rain. Halfway down the field, she saw a group of men carrying someone. She pushed forward, the rain drenching her as she reached them.

Her father shouted, "Marie, get inside! You'll get sick!"

"No, Da. I'm fine. Who is that?" she asked, breathless.

"A sailor," he said, his voice tight.

Marie bent down to look at the man, then turned to lead the group toward the house. Her heart raced. She felt alive, part of something important. It didn't matter if she grew worse—she needed to prove herself.

Inside, the men laid the sailor on the floor, his blood soaking into the earthen ground. Nora knelt beside him, her hands trembling as she assessed the splinter lodged deep in his thigh.

Marie stood beside her. Nora glanced up briefly, her voice low but rushed. "Marie, he's badly hurt. We need to get this splinter out."

Marie's hands trembled as she watched. "Will he die?" she whispered.

Nora didn't answer immediately. Her eyes flicked between the sailor's pale face and the splintered wood in his leg. The weight of the moment hung heavy in the room. Though she said nothing, the fear in her gaze told Marie everything she needed to know.

Marie Leads Men to the House

Afternoon

By afternoon, the ship lay on its side, broken and defeated, a wreck claimed by the sea. The storm had passed, leaving devastation in its wake. Twenty-two men lay dead on the beach, their bodies still and cold. Hundreds of Spanish survivors were scattered across the fields of Doona, many barely moving, exhausted from their battle with the sea. The long strand in Black Sod Bay was littered with wreckage.

The storm's rage had subsided, but tension lingered. The tide began to pull back, as if satisfied with its claim. Villagers moved quickly, offering blankets, tending to the shivering survivors, and carrying provisions to the stranded sailors.

Farrell moved through the wreckage with grim determination, his eyes scanning the horizon for unseen threats. He knew the danger wasn't over. Daniel McManamon, his hands raw from dragging debris, worked alongside his son Patrick, sorting through the scattered remains of the wreck. Supplies, personal belongings, and bodies lay strewn across the shore, each a grim reminder of the storm's fury. Daniel's heart was heavy as he worked, aware that these men were Spanish sailors—enemies of the English Crown.

Farrell approached, his voice low. "Set some of the provisions aside," he said, his sharp eyes flicking toward the horizon and then to the castle where Flynn and the soldiers worked.

"Flynn will be sniffing around," Farrell muttered, his gaze narrowing. "We must hurry. Grace O'Malley will be here soon."

The Pirate Queen, the Dark Lady of Doona, loomed in their thoughts. Flynn might hold temporary command in her absence, but it was Grace who held true power. Her arrival would decide the fate of the survivors, the provisions, and the future of all gathered here.

In the distance, Flynn barked orders, directing soldiers to launch two curraghs toward the wreck, hoping to salvage what they could—supplies, and anything of value.

Flynn and Farrell

Flynn's eyes scanned the beach with a scowl. Villagers worked quickly, pulling wreckage and supplies from the shore, ignoring him entirely. It infuriated him. In Grace O'Malley's absence, he was in charge, though no one seemed to acknowledge it.

"Daniel!" Flynn's voice cut through the wind.

Daniel McManamon straightened, his muscles tensing as he turned. "Flynn."

Flynn strode toward him, his boots sinking into the wet sand, anger darkening his face. "Ye're forgettin' who's in charge. This is O'Malley's land, and I'm her man while she's away. Ye'll take orders from me."

Daniel's eyes narrowed, his lips thinning. Flynn's gaze flicked down the strand. "Where's the man with the bloodied leg?"

"We've taken him to my house," Daniel replied.

Flynn's face flushed red. "Ye'll answer for this! Ye've no authority to take a Spaniard into yer home. They're dangerous, and ye're puttin' us all at risk!"

Daniel stepped forward, his voice low but firm. "Ye left that man to die, Flynn. Helpin' a wounded man is less dangerous than lettin' him die on yer watch. Want Grace O'Malley to hear about that?"

Flynn's eyes blazed, but before he could respond, Farrell stepped between them, his massive frame a wall of quiet authority.

"Enough," Farrell said, his voice low and steady, commanding the moment. His calm, unyielding gaze locked onto Flynn. "Daniel's right. We don't let men die, no matter where they're from."

Flynn, seething, stepped back but kept his tone harsh. "Underminin' my authority won't go unnoticed. If this goes wrong, it's on yer head, McManamon."

Farrell's voice turned cold. "Tell Grace whatever ye like, Flynn. We'll handle it. Strength doesn't come from lettin' men die. Now, see to yer own men."

Flynn glared but didn't push further. With a frustrated grunt, he turned and stalked back toward the shore, barking orders at his soldiers.

Uncle Farrell and Flynn

Respite

The crashing waves had faded to a distant roar, and the howling wind was now a low murmur. The beach lay quiet, its wreckage scattered like bones in the sand. Women moved like shadows, respectfully covering the bodies of the dead.

Inside Daniel and Nora's small house, the hearth's warmth did little to ease the lingering tension. The wounded Spanish sailor lay on a makeshift bed, his breaths shallow but steady. Nora sat beside him, dabbing sweat from his brow with trembling hands, her exhaustion mixing with the fading shock of the night. She glanced at Marie, asleep in the corner, the storm's toll evident on her pale face. The sight worried Nora, but there was no time to dwell.

Ronan sat slumped against the wall, staring into the fire. His chest rose and fell heavily, his limbs aching from the battle with the sea. But it was the weight of the night's events that truly wore him down. The faces of the men he'd dragged from the water haunted him—some lifeless, others clinging to him in desperation.

Nora watched her son, her heart aching for him. She crossed the room and knelt beside him, placing a gentle hand on his shoulder. "You did well tonight," she said softly.

Ronan's gaze stayed fixed on the fire, his jaw tightening. "It was scary, Ma," he admitted, his voice rough. "I didn't think I'd make it. I thought I'd drown out there."

Nora brushed a damp lock of hair from his forehead. "You were brave, Ronan. What you did tonight… it was more than most men could do."

Ronan turned to look at her, his eyes raw with exhaustion and emotion. She pulled him into an embrace, her arms steady around his trembling frame. "It's alright to be scared," she whispered. "We all were. But you faced it and did what had to be done. That's what matters."

Peggy, standing quietly by the door, stepped forward. "You're not really scared, are you, Ronan?" she asked softly.

Ronan gave her a tired smile. "I was, Peggy. But sometimes being scared is what keeps you alive."

Peggy nodded solemnly, leaning into Nora's side. Outside, the sea had calmed, but the tension among the people of Doona lingered. The night's events would not be forgotten.

The Sailor Wakes

In the early morning hours, the dim light of the hearth flickered, casting shadows across the room's rough stone walls. The air was heavy with the scent of damp earth and salt from the sea.

The wounded sailor lay near the window, his silhouette framed by dim light filtering through the curtain. His olive skin was tanned from months at sea, and a scar across his cheek told of battles past. His tattered Spanish naval doublet clung to his lean frame, and his boots, cracked and worn, rested beside the bed.

Rodrigo stirred, the dull ache in his leg pulling him from unconsciousness. His dry throat burned, and his mind flashed between the storm and the darkness that nearly claimed him. Opening his eyes, he winced, his hand instinctively moving to the splintered wood lodged in his thigh.

"Easy now," Nora's calm voice broke the silence. She knelt beside him, dabbing his brow with a damp cloth. Her brow furrowed with concern. "Ye've got a bad wound there. We'll need to tend to it soon."

Rodrigo groaned as he tried to sit, pain shooting through his leg. He fell back with a grimace. "Where... am I?" he rasped, his Spanish accent thick.

"You're in our home," Ronan replied, stepping closer. "We pulled ye from the sea. Ye almost didn't make it."

Rodrigo's memories returned in fragments—the storm, the shipwreck, his crewmates lost to the waves. His chest tightened. "The... others?" he managed to ask.

Nora and Ronan exchanged a glance. "Most survived," Ronan said cautiously. "But not all."

Rodrigo's eyes closed, his face shadowed with grief. The faces of his comrades flashed in his mind, the weight of the loss pressing heavily on him.

"Water," he whispered.

Nora brought a cup to his lips, and he drank greedily. Setting it aside, she looked at his wound. "We'll need to remove the splinter. It'll hurt, but if we don't, infection might kill ye."

Rodrigo nodded weakly. "Do it. I can take it."

Nora called softly, "Ronan, fetch yer father and Farrell."

Moments later, Daniel and Farrell entered, their expressions grim. The two men exchanged a look before Daniel spoke, "We'll hold ye steady. This'll hurt, but it's gotta be done."

Farrell's imposing frame knelt beside Rodrigo, bracing him. Ronan stood by the fire, watching anxiously. Nora prepared a sharp knife, heating it briefly in the flames.

"Hold him now," Nora instructed. Daniel and Farrell gripped Rodrigo's shoulders and legs. Rodrigo bit down on a cloth, bracing himself.

Nora worked quickly, slicing into the flesh to free the splinter. Rodrigo's body tensed, his muscles straining against the pain. His breaths came in ragged bursts, but he didn't cry out. Sweat streamed down his face as the knife cut deeper.

Finally, Nora pulled the splinter free. Rodrigo let out a strangled scream before collapsing into unconsciousness. Blood poured from the wound, and Nora moved swiftly to clean it, applying a poultice and wrapping it tightly with fresh bandages.

The room fell silent except for the crackling fire. Rodrigo was alive—for now. But the tension among them was palpable. They all knew his survival depended on the hours to come.

Lord Bingham

The stone fortress of Lord Richard Bingham, Governor of Connaught, loomed over the rugged western Irish landscape, its imposing structure built to withstand rebellion and storms. Inside, the cold stone walls were warmed by great hearths, the air thick with authority and the scent of burning wood. The fortress reflected its master: austere, unyielding, and focused.

Bingham stood by a narrow window, hands clasped behind his back, his sharp, pale eyes scanning the horizon. His thin gray hair and angular frame added to his severity. Known for his cruelty and discipline, Bingham's reputation stretched far beyond Connaught. He turned from the window, his embroidered doublet catching the light, a mark of his English refinement.

Beside him, his aide, Sir Christopher Hatton, hovered, his thin lips twisted in a sneer. Hatton's narrow eyes glinted with malice as he handed Bingham a sealed parchment. "Another report, my lord. More Armada ships wrecked."

Bingham broke the seal and scanned the report, his expression darkening. He crushed the parchment and threw it into the hearth. "Streedagh Beach," he muttered. "Several ships wrecked."

"Shall we dispatch the soldiers, my lord?" Hatton asked eagerly. "The Spanish survivors won't stand a chance."

Bingham's gaze turned icy. "More than that. The Armada's failure is God's gift, but these Spaniards cannot recover. Hunt them all down."

He strode to a large oak table, leaning over a map spread across its surface. His finger traced the coastline. "Issue an edict. Send word to every village from Sligo to Galway. Any Spanish survivor is to be executed. Anyone aiding them..." He paused, his eyes narrowing. "Will hang."

Hatton's sneer deepened. "A fitting punishment for the Irish rebels who defy English law."

"Indeed," Bingham said with a cold smile. "No mercy. Make it known."

Captain Edward Hamilton, a broad-shouldered officer with a scarred face, entered the room and saluted. "My lord, the troops are ready. Preparations for Streedagh Beach are underway."

"Good," Bingham replied. "Take two hundred men. Secure the beaches, scour the land, and kill any survivors. Leave no man standing."

"And the villages aiding survivors?" Hamilton asked.

"Burn them," Bingham said without hesitation. "Let it be a warning to all."

Hamilton saluted again, his face impassive. "As you command."

"And bring any survivors to me first," Bingham added. "They may have useful intelligence."

"Understood, my lord."

"We leave at once," Bingham commanded.

The sound of soldiers preparing for war echoed through the fortress as Bingham's men armed themselves. Outside, the grim march toward Streedagh Beach began, the governor's orders clear: leave no trace of defiance.

Governor Bingham's Mansion

Flynn orders Roadblock

Flynn paced the shoreline, his sharp eyes scanning the horizon where the wreckage of the Spanish Armada littered the beach. Though the storm had passed, its aftermath clung heavily to the village, dampening the spirits of those still working to salvage what they could. The sea had calmed, but Flynn's mind buzzed with tension, plotting his next move.

He turned abruptly, barking an order to his lieutenant. "Set the men on the road to Doona. No one gets through. I don't care who they are—farmer, traveler, or priest—no one comes within three miles of this shore."

The lieutenant, a wiry man with a scar down his cheek, saluted and hurried off. Flynn's face darkened as he watched him go. The Spanish sailors pulled from the wreckage were weak and injured, but Flynn knew they wouldn't go unnoticed for long. Lord Bingham would come, and the English had no mercy for Armada survivors or those who helped them.

Flynn strode to a cluster of men near overturned barrels. "Listen up," he barked. "Set a perimeter. Anyone on that road gets turned back or dealt with. And if they resist, you know what to do."

The men nodded, their expressions grim. One younger man hesitated, shifting uneasily. "And what about the families in the village? What if they see something?"

Flynn's sneer deepened. "Anyone who talks will regret it. For now, secure the road. No outsiders must know what's happening here."

The men exchanged uneasy glances but moved swiftly to their tasks. Flynn's voice cut through the mist. "Stay sharp. I'll not have Lord Bingham breathing down our necks because someone fell asleep."

As the men dispersed, Flynn stood watching, his mind racing. The Spanish survivors were a risk, but they could also be leverage if handled correctly. First, he had to ensure no word escaped Doona. This was his territory, and no one—not even Lord Bingham—would take it from him.

Marie Meets Rodrigo

The dim light of early morning filtered through the small window, casting soft shadows across the room. The house was quiet, save for the crackling of the hearth and the distant sound of the sea. Rodrigo lay motionless on his makeshift bed, his chest rising and falling with shallow breaths as the fever held him.

Marie stirred in her straw bed, weak but restless. She had slept most of the previous day, too drained from the storm to move. Yet, despite her exhaustion, she felt a flicker of hope, a purpose she hadn't known in weeks. Slowly, she pushed the blankets off, her frail frame almost swallowed by the heavy quilt. Her bare feet brushed the cold earthen floor as she sat up, breathing deeply to steady herself.

Her cheeks were pale, her chestnut hair loosely braided and spilling over her shoulder. Despite the toll of illness, her deep blue eyes reflected quiet determination. Wrapping her mother's old shawl around her shoulders, she stood, wobbling slightly, and took a few cautious steps across the room. Each movement was deliberate, a test of her strength, but her resolve carried her forward.

She crossed to where Rodrigo lay, his skin still hot with fever. The wound on his leg was swollen, but he appeared more at peace than before. Kneeling beside him, she brushed the damp cloth on his forehead, her touch gentle.

"Ma," Marie whispered, her voice soft but clear.

Nora stirred from her chair beside the hearth, blinking groggily. She rose quickly, moving to Marie's side. "Marie, you shouldn't be out of bed," she said, her voice filled with concern.

"I'm stronger now," Marie replied, her eyes fixed on the sailor. "I want to help. What's his name, Ma?"

Nora hesitated, then softened. "Rodrigo," she said.

Marie smiled faintly. "Rodrigo," she repeated, the name rolling softly off her tongue.

"Are you sure?" Nora asked gently. "You've been so ill."

"I need this, Ma," Marie said firmly. "He needs us. And I need to care for something. It helps."

Nora's chest tightened as she saw the flicker of life in Marie's eyes—a determination that hadn't been there in weeks. "All right," she said with a soft smile. "But rest too. Don't overdo it."

Marie nodded, her hand still resting on Rodrigo's forehead. Together, they worked in quiet harmony, tending to the sailor. Nora fetched fresh water and wrung out the cloths while Marie smoothed Rodrigo's blanket and whispered soothing words when he stirred.

For the first time in weeks, Nora allowed herself a glimmer of hope. Marie's illness had drained her, but now, beside Rodrigo, she seemed to find strength. Watching her daughter's gentle care, Nora saw a new light, fragile but growing.

Rodrigo stirred, his eyes fluttering open briefly. Clouded by fever, his gaze landed on Marie. He tried to speak, but only a faint groan escaped. Marie leaned in close, her voice soft. "Shh… it's all right. You're safe now."

Rodrigo's eyes closed again, his body relaxing. Marie stayed by his side, her heart steady, her purpose clear. For the first time in days, she felt like she belonged—like she was part of something larger than the illness that had tried to claim her.

The Courier for Bingham

The air around Doona was eerily still, the storm's aftermath leaving a quiet tension that clung to the village like a heavy fog. The sea had calmed, but an unsettled energy pulsed beneath the surface, as though everyone was holding their breath. Among the villagers and survivors, whispers spread of looming trouble—trouble far worse than the wrecked Spanish ships.

At the makeshift blockade Flynn had ordered, his men stood guard, their figures tense against the pale afternoon light. Weapons ready, they paced uneasily. Flynn had made it clear: no one was to come within three miles of the shore. But as the sound of hooves echoed in the distance, their resolve would be tested.

A lone rider appeared on the horizon, dressed in the formal colors of the English crown. He rode with purpose, his stern gaze fixed on the road ahead. Flynn's most trusted guard, Conall, stepped forward, his hand on his sword.

"Halt!" Conall barked. "This land belongs to Grace O'Malley. State your business."

The courier's posture stiffened. "I come from Lord Bingham, Governor of Connaught, with orders for all under his rule. Step aside."

Conall's jaw tightened. "No one passes without Flynn's word. Grace O'Malley rules here."

The courier scowled. "Lord Bingham's authority supersedes hers. Defy him, and you'll hang."

Conall remained firm. "You'll speak to Flynn. No further."

Moments later, Flynn emerged, his expression hard as he approached. His stomach sank at the sight of the Englishman. "What business does Lord Bingham have with us?"

The courier handed Flynn a sealed parchment. "By order of Lord Bingham, any Spanish sailors found are to be executed immediately. Anyone aiding them will face the same fate."

Flynn's hands clenched as he scanned the edict. It was worse than he feared. The punishment for helping the Spaniards wasn't just imprisonment—it was death for all, even women and children. The English soldiers were already moving toward Streedagh Beach, and it was only a matter of time before they reached Doona.

"Doona is under Grace O'Malley's protection," Flynn said, though his voice wavered.

The courier's sneer deepened. "Lord Bingham doesn't care. Protect the Spaniards, and you'll be branded a traitor. The choice is yours."

Flynn stared at the parchment, the weight of his decision pressing down. "You'll go no further. I'll send word to Lady O'Malley. She'll decide."

The courier gave a curt nod. "Don't delay. Lord Bingham won't wait." Turning his horse, he rode off. Flynn's heart pounded as he turned to his men.

"Send two riders to Rockfleet Castle," he ordered. "Grace must hear of this at once."

Conall hesitated. "The roads are treacherous, Flynn. The storm—"

"If they delay, Grace will have them swinging from her ship's yardarm," Flynn snapped.

Conall nodded and dispatched two riders. Flynn watched them disappear into the distance, the weight of the edict heavy on his shoulders. Each passing hour brought Bingham's soldiers closer, and without Grace, Flynn feared he would be forced to make a choice that could doom them all.

The Arrival of the Dark Lady of Doona

The day broke into rare beauty, the sea a deep blue stretching to the horizon under the golden light of early evening. The storm's chaos seemed a distant memory, though tension still clung to the village of

Doona. The sun burned through the clouds, and a stiff wind carried unease across the bay.

From the cliffs near Doona Castle, Slieve Mor Mountain cast a long shadow over the bay. Below, Grace O'Malley's ship approached with regal grace, its sleek hull cutting through the waves. The green banner with a golden crest of the O'Malley clan flew high from the mainmast, billowing in the wind.

Her crew worked swiftly as the ship prepared to dock, its towering black sails a defiant reminder of countless battles. On the battlements of Doona Castle, watchmen pointed as murmurs rippled through the gathered Spaniards taking refuge. Their faces showed uncertainty, their voices hushed with awe.

"Who is she?" one Spaniard asked.

"The Pirate Queen," another replied, reverent and fearful. "Grace O'Malley."

At the shoreline, news of her arrival spread quickly. Villagers rushed down, some excited, others wary. Grace's presence shifted the atmosphere. Her ship loomed larger, silhouetted against the evening sky. Small boats were prepared to meet her as she anchored offshore. The rhythmic crash of waves mingled with villagers' chatter and the whistling wind.

Grace stood at the bow, framed against the sea and sky. Her red hair, streaked with gray, blew in the wind as her ship rose and fell with the waves. She stepped onto the wet sand, her boots sinking momentarily before she strode forward, a commanding figure of land and sea. Her storm-colored eyes were sharp, her face weathered by years at sea, her beauty forged in strength and experience.

Dressed in a dark green shirt and worn trousers, with a crimson sash at her waist, Grace cut an imposing figure. A long leather coat billowed behind her, and two swords hung at her hips, their hilts gleaming. Her hand rested casually on one, a silent promise of readiness.

Behind her, rugged sailors and warriors fanned out—men who had followed her through storms and battles. They moved with purpose, their loyalty unshakable.

The crowd gathered on the shore parted as Grace approached, her presence magnetic and commanding. Every eye followed her, a mix of awe and fear. Her reputation had preceded her, and no one dared challenge her authority.

"Where is Flynn?" Grace called, her smooth voice cutting through the wind. There was no hesitation in her tone, only authority. The villagers remained silent, unsure how to react.

Richard Burke, her first mate, stood beside her, his scarred face and muscular frame a testament to years of battle and loyalty. He pulled at the oars of the small boat that had carried them ashore, his dark eyes scanning the gathered crowd.

Grace stepped from the boat, her boots splashing in the surf. The sun dipped low behind her, casting long shadows across the sand. She strode up the beach with purpose, the crowd parting before her. Behind her, her crew followed, their faces grim and determined.

The village seemed to hold its breath. Grace's arrival was not merely the return of a leader—it was the arrival of a force of nature. All who stood before her now waited, knowing their fates rested in her hands.

The Dark Lady of Doona

Grace Reacts

Grace O'Malley's piercing eyes swept over the gathered crowd as she strode up the beach, her jaw set with fierce determination. The villagers of Doona stood in tense silence, their breath collectively held as they awaited her response. Her reputation loomed larger than life—a ruler of these shores who answered to no one but herself.

Reaching the edge of the crowd, she stopped, her tall frame casting a long shadow in the fading light. Her men followed in formation, their presence as imposing as their leader. Grace's hands rested on the hilts of the twin swords at her hips, her fingers tapping lightly against the polished metal.

For a moment, only the sound of waves and the wind filled the air. Grace's sharp gaze moved from the villagers to the Spaniards huddled near the castle walls. Her expression was unreadable, calculating. She understood what had happened here—the rescue of these foreign soldiers—but she had yet to decide if it was an act of courage or folly.

Finally, she spoke, her voice low but powerful, cutting through the quiet. "So, you've taken in strangers, saved their lives, and risked your own. Admirable, some might say." Her words hung in the air, laced with both approval and warning.

Her eyes locked on Flynn, who stood near the front, his jaw clenched. Grace tilted her head slightly, a half-smile on her lips but without warmth. "I assume, Flynn, you had some hand in this. Or were these people acting without your guidance?"

Flynn shifted uneasily. "They took in the Spaniards against my advice, my lady," he said cautiously. "I thought it best to wait for your return."

Grace's smile vanished. "Wait? You thought to wait while lives were at stake?" Her words were calm, but the menace beneath them was unmistakable. Flynn paled, but Grace turned back to the villagers.

"The English are coming," she said, her voice steady and filled with quiet fury. "Bingham and his men will hunt these survivors, and when they come, they'll bring death to any who aided them."

A murmur ran through the crowd at the mention of Lord Bingham's name. Grace raised a hand, silencing them. "But this is my land, and I do not bend the knee to any English lord. These men are under my protection now, and any who defy that will face my wrath."

Her gaze turned to the Spaniards. "But make no mistake," she continued, her voice hardening. "If any of you harm my people or take advantage of this hospitality, I will see you cast back into the sea."

The Spanish captain, his face drawn with exhaustion, bowed his head in acknowledgment. The villagers exchanged glances, relief mingled with apprehension. Grace's promise came with conditions.

Satisfied, Grace turned to her first mate, Richard Burke, also known as The Devil's Hook. "Prepare the men," she said. "We may need to defend these shores before the night is over."

Burke nodded. "Aye, my lady. The men are ready."

Grace's gaze drifted out to sea, where the English would soon arrive. The villagers retreated to their homes, casting wary glances at Grace's anchored ship. The excitement of her arrival had been replaced by a growing sense of uncertainty.

As the sun dipped lower, Grace stood by the water's edge, her red hair billowing in the wind, her eyes fixed on the horizon. She was the Dark Lady of Doona, feared and respected, and tonight, her strength would once again be tested.

Marie Talks to Rodrigo

Marie sat beside Rodrigo, the fire's warmth barely reaching the corner where he lay. Her fingers trembled as she dipped a cloth into a basin of water, gently wiping the sweat from his brow. He stirred, his eyelids fluttering open for the first time, and his dark eyes locked onto hers.

"You're awake," she whispered, more to herself than him.

Rodrigo blinked, disoriented, his gaze drifting around the dimly lit room. "Where… am I?" His voice was a rough rasp.

"In our home," Marie said softly. "My father and brothers brought you here after the storm." She hesitated, unsure how much he understood through his heavy accent.

Rodrigo shifted slightly, wincing as pain shot through his leg. Marie reached out instinctively, her hand brushing his arm. The contact sent an unexpected jolt through her. "Don't move too much. You're still very weak." Her hand lingered a moment longer before she withdrew, her cheeks flushing in the firelight.

Rodrigo's eyes softened as they studied her, noting her pale complexion and trembling hands. "You... are ill?" he asked, his voice rough but curious.

Marie's smile was faint, tinged with sadness. "Yes. For a long time now." She twisted the cloth nervously. "But that doesn't matter. You're the one who needs help."

"It matters," he said quietly. "To you, it matters."

Her heart skipped at his words. No one had spoken to her like that before. She shook her head, deflecting. "I'm used to it. But you... you've come so far. After the ship..." She trailed off.

Rodrigo's expression darkened at the mention of the wreck but softened with a small smile. "We both survive... in our own ways." His gaze lingered, searching her face.

For the first time in years, Marie felt seen—not as the sick girl, but as someone who mattered. She swallowed hard. "I suppose we do."

A quiet fell between them, heavy yet comforting. When Marie reached to take the cloth from his forehead, her fingers brushed his hand—and this time, neither pulled away.

Grace O'Malley and Don Alonso's Deal

The air between Grace O'Malley and Don Alonso crackled with tension. The salty sea wind whipped around them, her fiery red hair flaring as she locked eyes with the Spanish captain. Behind her, Grace's men stood ready, loyal and armed. Flynn shifted uneasily, his gaze darting between Grace and Alonso.

"Half of what you've taken belongs to me," Grace said, her voice steady, one hand resting on her sword. "You're lucky to be alive. That's a gift I've granted you."

Don Alonso, worn from the wreck and aftermath, nodded. "Half it is, Lady O'Malley."

Before the deal could settle, Flynn stepped forward, frustration evident. "And what about the villagers, Grace? They've taken from the wreck. We should get it back."

Grace turned slowly, a faint smile playing on her lips. "Do ye not know the law of the sea, Flynn? They keep what they find. Besides," her voice dropped, sharp as a blade, "you've already taken most of it, haven't ye?"

Flynn scowled but held his tongue. "Farrell McManamon's hoarding a large stash," he muttered.

Grace raised an eyebrow. "Farrell, is it? I'll deal with him." Her tone carried an unspoken threat.

Don Alonso interjected diplomatically, "Perhaps they should keep only what they need."

Grace shot him a hard look. "They need more than they've taken, Captain. And you're lucky they didn't kill ye. On Clare Island, over seventy of your countrymen were slaughtered by islanders loyal to England."

Alonso stiffened, alarmed. "Did any survive?"

"No," Seamus, Grace's first mate, answered grimly.

Suspicion flared in Alonso's eyes. "How do you know this?"

Grace's lips curled. "I was there. Too late to stop it."

Alonso's brow furrowed. "What ship was it?"

Grace ignored the question, turning to Seamus. Alonso muttered to his men to note it, his eyes wary of her.

"You and your men will camp in the field between the castle and Fahy Church," Grace ordered. "You're not staying closer to shore."

She turned sharply to Flynn. "Take two men. Spread a rumor—Bingham's army should hear Spanish sailors are hiding near the Nephin Mountains. We need them away from the coast."

Flynn bristled but nodded, signaling two men to follow. They vanished into the darkening landscape.

Grace faced Alonso again, her red bandana fluttering in the wind. "This deal is your best chance, Don Alonso. These waters are treacherous—on land and sea. Tread carefully."

Alonso met her gaze, jaw tight. He knew he couldn't challenge her. "Understood," he said, bowing slightly.

Grace turned and strode back toward the castle, her men close behind. The storm had passed, but the real battle was just beginning.

The Pirate Queen and Don Alonso Agree

A Reflective Moment with Grace

The sky above Black Sod Bay blazed with the hues of dying daylight—fiery oranges, deep reds, and streaks of purple that mirrored the storm brewing inside Grace O'Malley. She stood alone atop the battlements of Doona Castle, the wind tugging at her red hair, whipping it like a banner of defiance. Below, the sea rumbled and hissed as if echoing the chaos in her mind.

Bingham was coming. The thought sharpened the edge of fear, and yet, Grace's heart remained steady. She had faced him before, faced death more times than she cared to count. But tonight was different. Tonight, as the light bled from the sky, she felt the weight of everything that had brought her to this moment.

Grace's eyes narrowed as memories unfurled, vivid and unbidden. She saw herself as a girl, standing in the shadow of her father, Eoghan O'Malley, as he led his fleet to sea. His voice, rough and strong, had carved the first lessons of leadership into her bones. *"The sea gives, but it also takes. If ye mean to rule it, you must be as relentless as the tide."* It was under his watch that she first learned how to fight, not just with swords, but with wit and cunning.

She recalled her first raid, the way her heart pounded as she led a small band of men to claim spoils from a rival clan. The roar of victory, the bloody wounds that marked her, the respect in the eyes of seasoned warriors when she returned—those moments forged her into more than just a chieftain's daughter. They birthed the Pirate Queen.

A sigh escaped her lips, carrying with it the ghost of her husband, Dónal O'Flaherty. He had been a man full of ambition, but his death taught her the harshest lesson of all: that power and loyalty were not always given freely. She earned every scar, every ounce of respect, by facing betrayal and death with unyielding resolve.

"Why do they follow me?" Grace muttered, eyes locked on the horizon. A storm was coming, the waves already swelling in anticipation. The answer rose within her like the sea itself: *Because they know I'll fight until my last breath to protect them, even against the impossible.*

And she thought of the countless times she'd stood before her men, sword in hand, her eyes blazing not just with rage, but with the unspoken promise that she would lead them through darkness and bring them back to the light. She remembered standing defiantly before Bingham once, the cold menace in his eyes, and how she had met his gaze without flinching, knowing that fear was a luxury she couldn't afford.

Grace's fist clenched as the first stars appeared, distant yet unwavering. She felt the past and present collide, a fire rekindling in her chest. She had come from the sea, fought to rule it, and now it was time to defend her realm and her people once more.

Turning from the setting sun, she whispered, "Let him come. He'll learn why they call me the Dark Lady of Doona."

Marie Rodrigo Outside

Later that night, when the house had fallen into a quiet slumber, Rodrigo shifted in his cot, the ache in his body pulling him from sleep. The fire had dwindled to embers, casting a warm glow across the room. He pushed himself upright, gritting his teeth at the pain in his side, and made his way to the door, leaning heavily as he stepped outside.

The chill of the night air prickled his skin, carrying the scent of salt and damp earth. The rhythmic sound of the tide whispered against the shore. Rodrigo stood there, breathing it in, letting the cool wind soothe his fevered body.

"Couldn't sleep?" a soft voice spoke from the shadows.

Rodrigo turned to see Marie sitting on a low bench near the edge of the porch, wrapped in a shawl. The moonlight illuminated her pale features, making her seem almost otherworldly.

"No," he admitted, his voice rough. He moved closer, settling beside her with a wince. For a moment, they sat in silence, listening to the tide.

"I come out here sometimes," Marie said quietly. "When the pain is too much or when I can't sleep. The sound of the sea calms me. It makes me feel like my illness is small compared to it."

Rodrigo nodded. "The sea is different in Spain," he said, his gaze on the dark waves. "The air is warmer, but its power is the same. A reminder that we're small pieces in a much greater world."

"Do you miss it? Your home?" Marie asked.

He hesitated, memories of sunlit afternoons and family laughter mixing with the chaos of the storm. "I do," he said softly. "But there's something about this place, too. Something I didn't expect."

Marie's heart quickened. "What did you expect?"

Rodrigo turned to her, his dark eyes searching hers. "Not this. Not someone who understands what it means to fight battles no one else sees. To survive when it feels impossible."

A silence stretched between them, filled with the soft roar of the tide. Marie's fingers tightened around her shawl. "I thought I'd never meet someone who didn't look at me with pity," she said, her voice trembling. "But with you… it feels different."

Rodrigo reached for her hand, his touch gentle. "It is different," he said, his thumb brushing over her knuckles. In that moment, their pain felt shared, more bearable.

For the first time, Marie believed she was more than her illness. As Rodrigo's grip tightened slightly, she felt a fragile hope bloom within her.

"I don't know what the future holds," Rodrigo said, his voice steady, "but I know that I want to face it here. With you."

Tears pricked Marie's eyes, but she smiled, determination sparking in her. "Then let's hope, Rodrigo. Let's hope for more."

They sat in silence, hands entwined, as the sea whispered its ancient songs, bearing witness to a bond taking root in the night.

Marie's Prayer

The wind outside the McManamon home whispered softly through the cracks in the wooden walls, a stark contrast to the raging storm they had survived days ago. Inside, the warmth of the fire mingled with a lingering heaviness. Marie sat upright in her bed, the ache in her limbs a constant reminder of her illness. Across the room, her mother, Nora, knelt beside Rodrigo, the wounded sailor. His breathing was shallow but steady, his life precariously held in her care.

Marie had been bedridden for weeks after a cold sapped her strength, confining her to her straw bed. The past winter had been cruel, with failed harvests and food shortages leaving her frail. Though summer had brought some recovery, she had not regained her strength and felt like a shadow of herself. She had forgotten what it meant to feel needed.

Now, with Rodrigo under their roof, something shifted within her. Caring for him gave her a renewed sense of purpose. For the first time in months, she felt a spark of life returning.

Nora moved to the small altar in the corner, where the family gathered each night for the Rosary. The statue of the Madonna, lit by flickering candlelight, offered comfort. Daniel knelt beside Peggy, who always stayed close to their mother, while Ronan leaned against the hearth, his strong frame weary.

Marie, determined to join them, pushed through her body's protests. She had missed many nights of prayer but felt compelled to be part of this moment. Slowly, she shifted to sit with her family, her trembling hands clutching her rosary.

As the family began their prayers, Marie noticed Rodrigo's gaze wander to the altar. His dark eyes softened as they locked on the Madonna. For the first time since he arrived, his face showed a flicker of peace. "Sí… Madonna," he murmured, his voice faint but reverent.

Nora glanced at him, surprised but calm. "You pray with us?" she asked gently.

Rodrigo nodded weakly. "Yes, I pray," he whispered in broken English, the words deliberate and meaningful.

Daniel passed him the rosary beads. Rodrigo took them with trembling hands, his strength barely sufficient to hold on. Together, the McManamon family and their unexpected guest prayed as one. The murmured prayers filled the room, the candlelight casting gentle shadows.

Marie whispered her Hail Marys, her heart focused on the Madonna. She prayed for strength—for herself, for Rodrigo, for healing and courage. A new, unspoken plea stirred within her: Let him stay. Let me heal, and let him heal too.

She opened her eyes briefly to see Rodrigo, his lips moving with the prayers, his focus unwavering despite his weakness. His struggle mirrored her own. For the first time in years, she felt hope where emptiness had reigned. She didn't fully understand her feelings but embraced them nonetheless.

As the Rosary ended, the family murmured a final "Amen." Nora approached Marie, brushing a gentle hand over her hair. "You're feeling better tonight," she said softly.

Marie nodded, her voice quiet but certain. "Yes, Ma. I am."

And for the first time, she believed it. A quiet strength was growing within her, and as she glanced at Rodrigo resting peacefully, she felt his presence might be part of what was bringing her back to life.

Marie prays for Rodrigo

Daniel and Don Alonso's Meeting

The Spanish sailors' camp quieted as evening fell, the men worn from their survival struggles and the negotiations with Grace O'Malley. Don Alonso stood at the edge, troubled by losses and uncertain about the future. The flickering campfires cast long shadows on the exhausted faces of his crew.

Alonso's gaze drifted as a figure approached, Daniel McManamon, moving carefully. Recognizing the importance of the villager, Alonso straightened.

Daniel stopped a few feet away, looking around. "Captain," he said in a low voice, "I need to speak with you, but it must stay between us."

Alonso's brow furrowed. He nodded for Daniel to continue.

"I found one of your men," Daniel said quietly. "He's badly injured, too hurt to move."

Alonso's heart raced. "One of my men? I thought they were all accounted for."

"He was washed ashore, separated from the others. He's in my house now, being cared for."

A surge of concern hit Alonso. "But my doctor is dead. No one can help him."

"He doesn't need a doctor," Daniel replied. "He needs time to heal. We're doing what we can."

Alonso's worry deepened. "Who is it?"

Daniel hesitated. "Rodrigo."

Alonso's face shifted from dread to disbelief. "Rodrigo? He's alive?" He paused, feeling a rush of relief. "I thought him lost to the sea."

Daniel nodded gravely. "He's in a fragile state. He can't move yet. It's best if no one knows—come tonight, after the camp settles."

Alonso understood. His gaze turned to the distant coastline, where Daniel pointed to a small house, its thatched roof barely visible in the twilight.

"I see it," Alonso murmured. "I'll come when the camp is quiet. No one will know."

Daniel nodded. "Keep it quiet, Captain. For everyone's safety."

Without another word, Daniel melted into the shadows, leaving Alonso to stare at the house where his loyal Rodrigo fought to survive. Determined, Alonso knew he would risk everything to save his man.

Rodrigo Visited by Don Alonso

The night had grown quiet, the only sound the soft crackling of the dying fire outside Daniel McManamon's house. Inside, the air was thick with tension and the scent of salt. Daniel waited by the door, listening for approaching footsteps. Ronan stood tense, while Nora sat beside Rodrigo, gently wiping his brow. Marie lingered near her mother, eyes on the wounded sailor, and Peggy hovered close to her.

A knock at the door. Daniel opened it to reveal Don Alonso and his second in command, their faces half-hidden in shadow. Alonso's sharp gaze scanned the room as he stepped inside.

"Good evening," Alonso said, his voice low but urgent.

Daniel nodded. "Captain."

Alonso immediately locked eyes on Rodrigo, lying pale and still. His breath caught before he knelt beside his man. "Rodrigo," he whispered, gripping his shoulder.

Rodrigo stirred, his eyes flickering open. Seeing Alonso, he smiled weakly. "Capitán…" His voice was faint but full of relief.

Alonso's eyes glistened. "Thank God you're alive," he murmured, his grip tightening slightly. "I thought we'd lost you."

Rodrigo nodded weakly. Alonso turned to Daniel and Nora, his face softening. "You've saved one of my finest men. I owe you a debt I can never repay."

Before Daniel could respond, Ronan stepped forward from the shadows. Alonso's gaze snapped to him. "You," he said, recognition dawning. "You pulled me from the sea."

Ronan nodded. "Yes, Captain. It was me."

Alonso studied the boy for a moment, his youthful appearance in stark contrast to the bravery he'd shown. A smile broke across Alonso's face. "I owe you my life, boy," he said. "You showed more courage than many seasoned sailors."

Ronan shifted, a small smile appearing. Alonso turned to Peggy, who stood beside her brother, peeking up at him. "What's your name?"

"Peggy," she replied shyly.

Alonso smiled. "You look after your family, don't you, Peggy?"

She nodded proudly. "Yes, Captain."

Alonso chuckled, easing the tension in the room before his gaze returned to Rodrigo's frail figure. His second in command stepped forward, grim. "We need to take him with us, Captain. It's too dangerous here."

Alonso nodded, brow furrowed. "Yes, he'll be safer in the camp."

"No," Daniel interjected, stepping forward. "He'll die if you move him now. He's too weak."

Alonso's face tightened. "But he can't stay here. It's not safe for him or your family."

Before Alonso could press further, Marie stepped forward, her voice steady and strong. "We'll take care of him," she said, meeting Alonso's eyes with determination. "He's improving. Moving him now will kill him."

Peggy quickly chimed in. "Yes, we'll take care of him."

Alonso hesitated, glancing between the sisters and then at Daniel. He saw the same resolve in their eyes that had saved his men. He sighed. "Alright," he said after a pause. "But we cannot leave him here forever. I'll come back for him."

"You have my word," Daniel replied. "When he's strong enough, you'll know."

Alonso nodded, glancing at his second in command. "We'll keep this quiet. But you must do the same."

With a final look at Rodrigo, Alonso turned to leave. As he reached the door, he paused, looking back at Ronan, Marie, and Peggy. "Take care of him. And thank you."

Ronan nodded, and with a final glance, Alonso and his second left into the night, leaving the McManamon family to care for their fragile secret.

Don Alonso Visits Rodrigo

News from Streedagh Beach

Streedagh Beach, Sligo

The following day dawned crisp and clear, the storm now a memory, but the tension lingered. Flynn's blockade on the road to Doona remained firm, though the men manning it were on edge. They had heard rumors—Lord Bingham's men were moving, and anyone aiding the Spanish survivors was in danger.

In the late morning, a lone rider approached the blockade. Cloaked in the greens and browns of the hills, his horse kicked up dust as it galloped toward the men. They tensed, hands tightening on their weapons, but one guard recognized him—a messenger loyal to Grace O'Malley.

"Let him through!" the guard barked, waving him forward.

The rider skidded to a halt just past the barricade, nodding in thanks before urging his horse onward, racing toward the castle. His urgency was clear as the pounding of hooves echoed across the fields.

At the castle gates, the rider dismounted swiftly and rushed to the heavy wooden doors, pounding on them with the flat of his hand. Flynn appeared, his expression hard.

"What is it?" he asked sharply.

"I've come from one of Grace O'Malley's ships," the rider replied, voice low and urgent. "There's word from Sligo. A rider is on his way with a message for Don Alonso."

Flynn's eyes flickered with surprise but he masked it quickly. "A message for the Spaniard?" he asked.

The rider nodded. "A Spanish galleon captain is searching for survivors. He's stationed south of Sligo."

Before Flynn could respond, the sound of more hooves thundering down the road grew louder. Another rider, wearing the colors of an English courier, approached the castle. Flynn's face darkened as the man dismounted with precision and strode toward the castle doors.

"I have a message for Don Alonso," the English rider said formally.

Flynn stepped aside, letting the man enter. Inside, the Spanish survivors, including Alonso, were gathered in the great hall. The room fell silent when the English rider entered. Alonso rose from his seat, eyes narrowing.

The rider handed Alonso a sealed letter marked with Lord Bingham's emblem. Alonso broke the seal and read quickly.

"A captain of a galleon is south of Sligo," Alonso murmured, repeating the earlier message. "He's searching for survivors of the Armada."

"How many wrecked ships?" Alonso asked, eyes rising from the letter.

"At least ten ships between Donegal and here," the rider replied grimly. "There are more to the south—many more. Three were destroyed at Streedagh beach, killing thousands. I saw the bodies."

Alonso's face went pale, but his jaw clenched in determination. "What of the survivors?"

The rider's voice grew low with anger. "Lord Bingham saw them too. Seventy-seven men survived, but they were hanged on a scaffold above the beach that evening."

Silence fell. The weight of the news pressed heavily on everyone. Alonso's hands shook as he lowered the letter, the enormity of the tragedy sinking in. His men exchanged uneasy glances.

Alonso turned to Flynn, voice hard. "If Bingham's men are executing survivors, we don't have much time. We need to secure our provisions and leave before they find us."

Flynn nodded slowly. "Grace O'Malley's men are with us. We'll spread the rumor, sending Bingham's forces toward the Nephin Mountains. But you must be quick, Alonso. Bingham's reach is long."

Alonso turned to his second-in-command, voice filled with resolve. "We leave tonight. Gather the men and prepare them. We won't wait for the English to come for us."

As the men moved into action, the looming threat of Bingham's wrath pushed them forward. The race against time had begun.

The Hangings at Streedagh Beach, in Sligo

Flynn's Men Return

Grace paced the stone floor of the castle's main hall, her boots echoing with each step. The torches on the walls cast dancing shadows, making her appear even fiercer. Flynn and her first in command, Dónal, stood nearby, faces taut with tension. The storm outside had passed, but the storm inside was just beginning.

By afternoon, Flynn's men returned, breathless from their reconnaissance. They were cold, dirty, and tired, but urgency filled their voices.

"Bingham's army is on the march," one man panted, collapsing onto a bench. "Over fifty men, comin' from Bangor. But they took the bait—heading toward the Nephin Mountains, looking for Spaniards."

Grace didn't stop pacing, nodding sharply. The plan had worked, but rumors of the wreck at Doona had already reached Bingham's men.

"Bingham heard about the wreck here," the man continued. "Talk of Spaniards washing ashore. We don't have much time."

Grace halted, her gaze snapping to Flynn and Dónal. "We're in great peril," she said, voice low and fierce. "Bingham's not a fool. If he smells blood, he'll tear this place apart."

Flynn swallowed hard. "What do we do, Grace?"

She clenched her jaw, mind racing. The news of Bingham's march and the wreck at Doona had put them in an impossible situation. She turned sharply. "Call Don Alonso. He needs to hear this."

Soon after, Don Alonso entered the hall, his face pale and saltwater-stained. He approached Grace, Flynn, and Dónal.

"Señora O'Malley," he said, nodding respectfully. "What news?"

Grace's eyes locked onto his. "There is no way out of here, Alonso. Bingham's army is closing in, and they'll be here within days. We need to make our move now."

Don Alonso's face tightened, his brow furrowing in concern. "What can we do?"

Grace walked to the window, eyes on the sea. The wreckage of Alonso's ship bobbed lifelessly in the waves, a sad emblem of their destruction. On the shore, the bodies of twenty dead Spaniards lay, hastily covered. It was only a matter of time before Bingham's men uncovered the truth.

Grace's gaze darkened. "We need to burn the ship. Immediately."

"Burn it?" Alonso's face showed shock. "But why?"

"I don't want Bingham or his men to know the true size of your vessel," Grace said. "We'll tell them the castle crew killed most of the sailors when they came ashore. We'll scatter the bodies, burn the ship, and claim the survivors fled south."

Dónal's brow furrowed. "And what do we do after that, Grace? What about Bingham's army?"

"We tell Bingham his prey is gone," she replied. "He'll be suspicious, but we'll give him a show. Scatter the dead along the shore, swords plunged into their bodies, like a battle took place."

Flynn's face paled. "Farrell McManamon took a hoard from the ship. What about the villagers? They've taken treasure. What if Bingham's men start asking questions?"

Grace's eyes narrowed. "The law of the sea, Flynn—do ye not know it? The villagers keep what they've found. You've gotten most of it, haven't you?"

Flynn hesitated. "Aye, most of it… but Farrell—"

"I'll speak with Farrell," Grace cut him off. "Leave that to me."

Alonso, still processing Grace's plan, spoke up. "The villagers should keep only what they need."

Grace shot him a hard look. "Don Alonso, they need more than what they've taken. You're lucky they didn't kill you when you washed ashore. Not far from here, on Clare Island, over seventy Spaniards were put to death by the locals—loyal to England."

Alonso stiffened, alarm creeping into his eyes. "Killed? All of them?"

"Aye, all of them," Grace replied, voice cold. "I arrived too late."

Dónal, sensing the tension, nodded slightly in understanding. Grace didn't regret much, but the massacre on Clare Island haunted her. It was a brutal reminder of the world they lived in, and she wouldn't let it happen again.

Alonso's suspicion grew. "How do you know so much about this?"

Grace met his gaze, voice sharp as steel. "Because I was there. And this time, I'll not let it happen again."

Alonso, still unsettled but trusting her resolve, nodded. "What do you propose we do in the meantime?"

Grace looked back out the window, watching the waves. "You and your men will camp in the field between the castle and Fahy Church for now. We'll get you out of here as soon as we know where Bingham is."

Santa Maria Encoronada Burning

A Ship at Elly Bay

The morning air was thick with tension as a small group of men approached Grace O'Malley's castle. The first light of dawn barely touched the sky, and the winds had stilled, but the storm of urgency had only just begun.

Inside, Grace stood with Flynn, Alonso, and Ronan. The men burst in, breathless and dripping with seawater. "There's a ship anchored in Elly Bay," one of them said. "Spanish. The Duquesa Santa Ana."

Alonso's eyes widened. "Two days' march," he muttered, calculating the distance.

Flynn was less optimistic. "Marchin' north is a fool's errand," he said. "Bingham's men are everywhere. You'll be dead before you get near the ship."

Alonso's face darkened, but Grace cut in, her voice firm. "There's no time to send a rider. Bingham's closing in, and we don't have days to wait."

Flynn sneered. "You're sending them to their deaths, Grace."

Grace stepped closer. "What would you have me do, Flynn? Wait for Bingham to trap us? Watch him burn this castle and hang Alonso and his men? I won't give him that victory."

The room fell silent.

Alonso looked at Flynn, then back at Grace. "How will we even know the way?"

After a pause, Ronan stepped forward. "I'll lead them," he said. "I know the way through the bogs. Bingham's men won't find us there."

All eyes turned to Ronan. Daniel, standing in the shadows, looked at his son with a mix of pride and fear. Ronan wasn't just volunteering—he was stepping into something that would change him forever.

Grace studied him closely, then nodded. "We'll travel by night. It's the only way to avoid the patrols."

She pulled out a small iron cross, familiar to the old symbols of St. Brigid, and handed it to Ronan. "Take this. You'll need all the luck you can get."

Ronan took the cross, feeling its weight. His fingers tightened around it. This wasn't just a mission—it was his moment. He wasn't a boy anymore. He was leading men through danger, where death waited in every shadow.

"I'll do it," he said, his voice stronger. There was no turning back.

Grace nodded once, then turned to Alonso. "Gather your men. We leave tonight. Every hour we wait, Bingham gets closer. And if we're caught, there will be no mercy."

Alonso nodded, glancing at Ronan with a flicker of admiration. "We'll be ready."

As the camp stirred into action, Flynn barked orders, men gathered their things, and horses were readied. Ronan stood still for a moment, staring down at the iron cross in his hand. The responsibility settled over him like a heavy cloak, but there was comfort in it. He wasn't just following orders anymore—he was leading.

With a final glance at the horizon, where the first light of dawn touched the sky, Ronan set his jaw. He wasn't a boy anymore. The journey ahead was dangerous, but he knew this was his moment.

Grace said, "You will leave tonight, as soon as the sun goes down."

Mary McBride

The late afternoon sun cast a warm glow over the rugged path to Fahy Church. The McManamons, along with other villagers, walked together, their voices mingling with the breeze and the distant crash of waves against Black Sod Bay. Mary McBride, her auburn hair tied back, walked at the edge of the group. Her eyes flicked between her family and Ronan, who was several paces ahead, talking animatedly with his father, Daniel.

Mary's heart fluttered as she watched him. The stories had spread—how Ronan had guided Don Alonso and his men, showing bravery when the storm had nearly claimed them all. She'd known Ronan since childhood, but today, with his bravery fresh in her mind, he seemed different—older, stronger, more like the man she hadn't realized she wanted to see in him.

The path narrowed, and she found herself walking beside him. Ronan turned, a smile breaking across his face. "Mary! Didn't see ye there. How've ye been?"

She swallowed, willing her voice not to betray her racing heart. "Ah, well enough, Ronan. I hear ye've been braver than all the heroes of old."

Ronan chuckled, light but dismissive. "Stories grow bigger with every tongue they pass. 'Twasn't half as grand as they say."

Mary's fingers tightened around the wildflowers she carried. "Still, 'tis not every lad who can say he's stood with Spanish captains and weathered the storms."

Ronan's eyes shifted ahead to the distant Fahy Church. "Aye, but there's no time for thinking of that now. We've more pressing matters."

As they neared a rocky patch, Mary's steps faltered, and she reached out instinctively, her fingers brushing his arm. The touch was brief, but enough to make her cheeks flush.

Ronan glanced down at her, brows furrowing. "Ye alright, Mary?"

She forced a laugh, though it sounded strained. "Aye, just a stone in my path. Nothing more."

They walked in silence, the voices of their families and neighbors drifting around them. Mary's heart ached with the quiet. To him, she was still just the childhood friend who once beat him in a race across the sand.

Ronan slowed, turning back to her. "Busy now, Mary. We'll talk soon, aye?" He gave her a quick smile before stepping ahead to join Daniel and the others.

She nodded, her words stuck in her throat. "Aye, soon," she whispered, watching him walk away. The space between them felt wider than ever.

As they neared the church, the sun cast long shadows, and Mary glanced at the wildflowers in her hand. Crumpled now, she loosened her grip, feeling the sting of realization. She saw him in a new light, but to him, she was still only the past.

The Mass at Fahy

Fahy Church, Ballycroy

The evening sun cast a golden hue over Doona's landscape, transforming the rugged beauty of the Irish countryside into something sacred. Slieve Mor, standing tall in the distance, watched over Black Sod Bay, and the crumbling stone walls of Fahy Church rose like a memory of a time gone by. This ancient place, now reclaimed by nature, was chosen for a Mass that would unite the people of Spain and Ireland in prayer amidst the wreckage of war and loss.

Alonso stood by the stone wall, his dark eyes scanning the gathered crowd. His men, many still nursing wounds, stood in a rough line near a simple wooden altar adorned with a white cloth. The priest, ready to offer Mass for both the living and the dead, stood at the front.

Grace O'Malley arrived with her crew, her commanding presence drawing attention as her men stood behind her like silent guards. The O'Malley banner fluttered in the stiff wind. Grace had agreed to Alonso's invitation but insisted on holding the Mass at Fahy Church, a place with its own history.

The villagers, few but strong, stood in quiet reverence. Among them were Daniel, Nora, Ronan, and little Peggy, her small frame barely moving in the wind. Marie, too weak to walk, sat propped up by the altar, her hands resting in her lap, watching the scene unfold. She prayed for Rodrigo's healing and for the stirrings in her heart. Would he stay? Could he?

As the priest began the Mass, his Latin words rising above the wind, Alonso glanced at Grace, who stood with her crew at the back. Grace, her red hair held back by a bandana, stood with arms crossed, her gaze never leaving the ceremony. Her first mate, Cormac MacTavish, stood beside her, his loyalty evident.

The wind carried the smell of the sea. In the distance, the skeletal remains of the Spanish ship shifted with the waves, a broken husk, scattered across the shore. The dead still lay around it, their bodies either buried in the sand or washed up on the banks, reminders of the storm that had claimed them.

As the Mass reached its height, with the host raised high, a silence fell over the gathering. Even the wind seemed to hold its breath. Peggy, standing near the altar, clasped her hands together, whispering her own prayers, unaware of how deeply her innocent presence moved those around her.

The sun began to set, casting a warm glow over the scene. The mountains, the bay, and even the shipwreck seemed bathed in an ethereal light. It was a brief moment of peace amidst the uncertainty and danger ahead.

As the Mass ended and the priest lowered the chalice, Alonso's first officer, Ascoli, approached. His voice was tense as he reported to Alonso. "Six soldiers, unaccounted for. They're missing."

Alonso's face darkened. He knew of one—Rodrigo, hidden safely at Daniel's house. That left five. Missing soldiers were often deserters.

"Deserters, most likely," Alonso muttered, though Grace, standing nearby, overheard.

As the last rays of sun dipped below the horizon, Grace turned to Alonso, her eyes sharp. "Whatever their fate, Captain, let's hope they don't bring trouble our way. There's enough of it already."

"They are out of my hands, I'm afraid," Alonso said. He turned to his officer. "Get all the men ready. We leave as soon as darkness descends."

The people began to disperse, unaware that the soldiers would be gone by morning.

Mass at Fahy Church

A Farewell Before the Journey

As the sun dipped lower, casting an orange glow over the land, Ronan stood outside his home, his heart heavy with the weight of his impending departure. The familiar sounds of the farm—the lowing of the cow, rustling leaves, and distant waves—filled the air, but tonight everything felt different, laced with sorrow. He glanced toward the fading sun, knowing he wouldn't see it set here again for some time.

The door creaked open, and Ronan turned to see his mother, Nora, stepping out, wiping her hands on her apron. Peggy followed, her face tight with worry. Inside, Marie and Catherine watched, concern in their eyes as their brother prepared for what could be a perilous journey.

Nora approached him, wrapping her arms around him in a tight embrace. "Ye come back to us, Ronan. Safe and sound, ye hear? Ye're a brave lad, but don't be takin' unnecessary risks." Her voice trembled, and she wiped away a tear with the back of her hand.

"I'll be back before ye know it, Ma," Ronan replied, his voice cracking slightly. "Besides, I'll be with Don Alonso and the others. We'll take care of each other."

Peggy stepped forward, clinging to his leg. "Ye're not really goin', are ye?" she whispered.

Ronan knelt, ruffling her hair gently. "I have to, Peg. But don't worry, I'll be back soon enough. And I'll bring ye somethin' from Sligo."

Peggy nodded, but the tears in her eyes betrayed her. Marie and Catherine joined in, offering hugs, their faces pale with concern. Marie, though weak, stood tall and pressed her cheek to Ronan's in a wordless farewell.

As Ronan adjusted his satchel, he noticed a shadow at the edge of the yard. He squinted and saw Mary McBride approaching, her figure barely visible in the fading light. She moved hesitantly, hands clasped together nervously.

Ronan's brow furrowed in confusion. He had known Mary for years, but something about her seemed different today. Her auburn hair was braided back, and her eyes, clear and focused, were locked on him.

"Mary?" he asked, standing straighter. "What brings ye here?"

Mary stepped closer, cheeks flushed. "I wanted to wish ye well, Ronan. I heard ye were leavin' with the Spaniards, and I thought ye might need somethin' to keep ye safe."

Ronan blinked in surprise as she held out a small stone cross, its surface smoothed by careful hands. "I made it meself," she said softly. "I thought ye might need a bit of extra protection."

Ronan stared at the cross for a moment, warmth spreading through him. "Thank ye, Mary. It's... perfect."

She smiled shyly, her face lighting up. "Keep it close, Ronan. And come back safe, alright?"

Ronan nodded, slipping the cross into his satchel. "I will. I promise."

Just then, the deep voice of Uncle Farrell boomed from behind. "Ah, lad, there ye are." Farrell strode up, a large pistol in his hand. "Take this," he said, pressing the weapon into Ronan's hand. "Ye'll need it where ye're goin'." He shoved a satchel into Ronan's arms, heavy with Spanish gold coins. "In case ye run into trouble, or need to barter with a soul."

Ronan stared at the pistol and gold. "Uncle, I don't—"

"Ye'll take it," Farrell interrupted, clapping him on the shoulder. "Ye're a McManamon. We always come prepared."

Ronan adjusted the weight of the gifts and turned to face his family and Mary one last time. The sun was nearly gone, casting the world in twilight. The old cow let out a low moo, and Ronan chuckled despite himself. "I won't be missin' ye," he muttered, glancing at the animal.

With a final embrace from his mother, a quiet nod from Mary, and a firm handshake from Farrell, Ronan turned and began to walk down the path, his heart heavy and light. The journey ahead was full of danger, but for the first time, he felt a new sense of purpose, bolstered by the small cross and the quiet promise of someone waiting for him when he returned.

Mary Gives Ronan a Cross

The Journey

As the sun dipped below the horizon, Ronan, Alonso, and their men moved silently along the jagged rocks, the sea whispering behind them. The air was thick with tension as they made their most perilous journey yet—past Ross Point, the sharp edge of their escape.

Ronan, seventeen but bearing the weight of a man, led the column of over 250 survivors. No torches illuminated their path. The only sound was the soft crunch of their boots on the rocks and the steady breath of men moving like shadows across the cliffs.

Alonso followed Ronan closely, trusting the boy's instincts. The English patrols were hunting them, and if caught, it would be a massacre.

Ronan stopped abruptly, signaling the others to halt. His heart pounded as he crouched low, motioning for Alonso to join him. In the distance, dim light flickered through the trees—an English encampment.

Ronan's pulse quickened. He counted at least twenty soldiers, their campfires barely visible. They were relaxed, unsuspecting.

"How do we get past them?" Alonso whispered.

"We must kill them," Ronan replied, his voice steady. "If we attempt to bypass them, it'll end in disaster."

Alonso hesitated. "How?"

"We attack just before they change their watch," Ronan suggested. "They'll be tired, unprepared."

Alonso nodded, his hand gripping his sword. "We'll strike from all sides—quick and silent."

The men waited for the right moment. The moon climbed higher, casting a silver hue over the coastline. The English soldiers, unaware, yawned and stretched.

Ronan gave the signal. The men surged forward, like wolves in the night. Swords flashed in the dim light, and the crack of steel against flesh echoed through the air. The soldiers had no time to react before they were cut down.

Ronan, agile and swift, engaged an Englishman who slashed at him. He ducked under the blade and drove his knife upward, catching the man in the ribs. The soldier fell silently.

Amid the chaos, Alonso slipped on the rocky ground. A soldier loomed over him, sword raised, ready to strike. Ronan saw it in a flash and fired his pistol. The shot rang out, and the English soldier crumpled to the ground, the sword falling from his hand.

Alonso gasped, looking up at Ronan with wide eyes. "You saved me again."

Ronan, still holding his smoking pistol, nodded, his hand trembling slightly. "Aye, Captain. I did."

With the last of the soldiers overpowered, the camp fell silent. But there was no time to rest. Thirteen English soldiers were bound and gagged, their faces pale with fear.

Ascoli, Alonso's first officer, approached with a dark glint in his eyes. "What shall we do with them, Captain?"

"They should be silenced if we are to survive," Ascoli continued, his voice cold.

Ronan's gut tightened. He didn't want to kill in cold blood. Alonso met Ascoli's gaze, his jaw tight. "No. We leave them. Tie them up. We need one more day."

Ascoli hesitated. "Captain, if even one escapes—"

"They won't escape," Alonso interrupted. "We'll leave them here."

The soldiers quickly bound the Englishmen and extinguished the campfire, leaving them under guard. Ronan wiped the sweat from his brow, his chest heavy with the weight of their decision.

"One more day," Ronan murmured, echoing Alonso's words. But the tension in his chest remained. One slip, and everything could be lost.

"Onward," Alonso said quietly. "We make for Ross Point."

The group moved into the night, leaving behind the bodies and the bound soldiers as the tide began to rise, washing away the evidence of their battle. The journey ahead was still fraught with danger, but for now, they had survived another deadly encounter.

Captain Alonso and Ronan Lead Men Away in Time

Bingham's Troops

The sun dipped lower in the sky as the tide receded, exposing the wreckage scattered along Black Sod Bay. The remnants of a Spanish galleon lay twisted in the sand, its shattered hull creaking in the wind. Dead soldiers, half-buried in seaweed and debris, littered the shoreline like broken driftwood. The air was thick with the smell of salt and decay.

Two English ships anchored in the bay, Bingham having traveled on one, and Captain Comerford on the other. It had taken hours to unload the soldiers, surprising the villagers who had expected them by land.

Lord Richard Bingham marched across the beach with measured steps, each one sinking into the damp sand. His sharp blue eyes took in every detail—the fragments of wood, the broken weapons, the bodies strewn across the shore. His face, hardened by years of command, was etched with deep lines, his mouth set in a thin, unyielding line.

His gray hair, cut short, whipped in the wind, though he remained unmoved. A long leather coat billowed behind him, his sword glinting in the pale light, a symbol of the power he wielded. He stepped over a corpse, barely glancing at it. Mercy was weakness, and weakness had no place in his world.

"Search every inch of this beach," he barked, his voice cutting through the roar of the waves. A soldier nodded and hurried to relay the order. Bingham's gaze turned toward the horizon, where the last fragments of sunlight clung to the sky, fighting against the approaching storm clouds. His mind was already calculating—no emotion, just the cold efficiency of a man who saw every loss as a path to control.

Behind him, Captain Comerford's tall figure cast a shadow across the sand. His expression mirrored Bingham's, disdain etched in every line of his face as he surveyed the wreckage.

Red-coated soldiers fanned out across the beach, their boots sinking into the wet sand. They prodded the wreckage with spears, turning over pieces of debris, kicking at bodies in search of anything useful. Their movements were mechanical, the mood grim—this was a scene of death and defeat, but Bingham's focus was only on what he could still gain.

Lord Richard Bingham

Bingham's Soldiers Inspect the Dead

The Healing

The morning sun filtered weakly through the windows of Daniel and Nora's cottage, casting long shadows across the uneven floor. The fire in the hearth crackled softly, barely enough to keep the chill at bay. Inside, the room was quiet except for the occasional groan of Rodrigo, lying in the corner on a makeshift bed.

Rodrigo's leg, still bandaged, was propped up on straw pillows. His dark hair clung to his brow, and his olive skin had regained some color, but he remained gaunt, a reminder of the ordeal he'd barely survived.

Marie knelt beside him, dipping a rag into saltwater to clean the festering wound on his leg. Her auburn hair, once vibrant, hung loose around her pale face. She had been bedridden not long ago, but caring for Rodrigo seemed to rekindle her spirit.

Rodrigo winced as the saltwater stung his wound, a low groan escaping his lips. He glanced at Marie and managed a small smile, despite the pain. "It's alright," he whispered, "you're helping me, even if it hurts."

"Sorry," Marie whispered, her voice steady but soft. "We have to clean it, or it'll get worse."

Rodrigo gripped the edge of the bed, enduring the pain. Even in his weakened state, his strength remained. His dark eyes lingered on Marie before he closed them again.

Peggy and Catherine flitted around the room, doing small tasks. Peggy, ever curious, hovered by Rodrigo's side, fascinated by his tales of faraway lands.

"Marie," Peggy piped up, "Do ye like him?"

Marie froze, heat rising to her cheeks. "What do ye mean, Peggy?" she asked, though her blush betrayed her.

Peggy leaned in closer. "I see the way ye look at him! Do ye think he'll stay with us?"

Marie's heart raced, but before she could answer, Catherine nudged Peggy with a grin. "Peg, hush now," she scolded, though amusement flickered in her eyes.

Nora, stirring the pot of oats by the hearth, glanced over her shoulder with a knowing smile. She'd seen the change in Marie since Rodrigo's arrival—the light returning to her daughter's eyes. Maybe this was the healing Marie needed after her long illness—someone to care for, a reason to hope.

Rodrigo shifted in bed, his face tight with pain. Marie hurried to his side, adjusting the crutch Daniel had made for him. "Don't push yourself," she murmured. "Ye're not ready yet."

Rodrigo sighed in frustration. "I need to walk," he rasped. "I can't stay here forever."

"Ye will," Marie replied softly, steadying him. "But ye need time."

Their eyes met, a bond forming between them in shared pain and recovery. For a brief moment, there was something more than words could express. Marie's heart fluttered, and she turned her attention back to his wound, brushing her hand over the bandage.

At that moment, Daniel entered the room, his broad form filling the doorway. He nodded at Rodrigo. "Ye're makin' progress, lad. A slow battle, but ye'll win it yet."

Rodrigo's dark eyes flickered with gratitude. "I owe you all much," he said quietly. "Without your family... I wouldn't be here."

Daniel waved him off. "No need for thanks. Just keep gettin' stronger. We've lost too many men to the sea." His tone turned serious. "What happened out there, lad? What happened to the Armada?"

Rodrigo shifted in bed, his face darkening at the mention of the Armada. "We were torn apart by the storm," he said slowly, his voice rough. "Most of the fleet never made it to England. The storm was our downfall."

Daniel nodded solemnly, glancing at the girls, who listened intently. "Aye. We'll help ye get back to yer men when the time comes," he said. "But for now, rest. Ye've still a ways to go."

Rodrigo lay back, exhaustion evident, but his eyes remained on Marie. There was something unspoken between them, something shared. As Daniel turned to leave, Peggy tugged at his sleeve.

"Da," she whispered, "do ye think Rodrigo will stay with us?"

Daniel looked at her, then at Rodrigo, and his gaze softened as he looked at Marie, who lingered beside him. "That's not for us to decide, Peg," he said gently. "But maybe he's found more here than he expected."

Marie's heart pounded as her father left the room. She stayed by Rodrigo's side, adjusting his blanket. His dark eyes, though tired, were soft as he looked at her. A faint smile tugged at his lips, and for the first time in a long while, Marie felt a glimmer of hope. Perhaps there was more waiting for her than she had once thought.

Grace and Bingham Face Off

The wind screamed through the stone walls of Grace O'Malley's castle. She stood atop the battlements, her eyes narrowed at the scene below. Redcoats swarmed the beach, rifles slung over their shoulders, kicking through the wreckage. Dead Spaniards lay scattered like driftwood. And there was Bingham—rigid, as if he owned everything beneath his gaze. Beside him, Comerford gestured sharply.

Had they fooled them?

Grace's heart hammered. She spun and descended the stairs, boots echoing off the stone. Richard Burke appeared at her side, hand on his sword hilt.

"Summon the men," she snapped. "All of them. Assemble in the courtyard. We need to look stronger than we feel."

Burke vanished, and the wind outside rose, carrying the salt stink of death from the sea.

By the time she stepped into the courtyard, her men had formed ranks. Rough, scarred, and determined. Swords glinting, armor battered but steady.

The crunch of boots came from beyond the gate—Bingham and his men approaching. The courtyard stilled as the gates swung wide. Bingham and Comerford entered, flanked by fifty redcoats in perfect lines. Grace folded her arms, her eyes as cold as the sea air.

Bingham began, his voice dripping disdain, "Lady O'Malley, where are they?"

"Who?" Grace's voice was steel.

"The Spaniards. I know they're here."

"They're gone," Grace replied. "Escaped to the south in the storm. I arrived too late."

Bingham stepped closer, eyes narrowing. "And the dead on the beach?"

"The peasants killed them—and some of my men from the castle. Before the storm swept the rest away."

Bingham's lips thinned. "How did they escape?"

Grace didn't blink. "I told ye, Lord Bingham. I wasn't here."

Bingham studied her. "And none of your own lie dead there?"

Grace's heart pounded, but her face remained ice. "Three of my men from the castle died. We buried them at sea."

"Three?" Bingham's eyes narrowed. "How convenient."

"Aye. That's how it goes."

The wind howled through the stones. Comerford stepped forward, voice dripping malice. "If you're lying, Grace, it won't just be your men who suffer."

Grace's jaw tightened. "Search if you like, Comerford. You'll find nothing."

Bingham glanced at Comerford, suspicion twisting his face. He turned sharply, barking orders. "Search every inch. Scour the beach. Turn every rock."

The redcoats moved quickly, rifles at the ready. Grace watched, fists clenched. They couldn't know the truth—that some had escaped, hidden under her watch.

Bingham turned back to her. "We camp here tonight. We'll search until satisfied. And if I find you've lied..." He leaned in, voice low, "I'll see this castle burn."

Grace held his gaze, her face stone. "You'll find nothing, Bingham."

They locked eyes. The air vibrated with hatred. One wrong move—and blood would spill.

Bingham turned on his heel, motioning for Comerford to follow. Their soldiers marched out, boots echoing in the silence they left behind.

The gates closed. Grace exhaled, slow and measured. She had played her hand. Now, she had to see if it would hold.

Comerford and Bingham

Dawn, Blacksod Bay

Aboard Bingham's Ship

Captain Gerald Comerford emerged from the shadow of the ship's mast, his silhouette unmistakable against the fading light of the day. He was a tall, imposing figure, his battered tricorn hat casting a shadow over his weathered features. The patch over his right eye gave him an air of danger, as if every scar and every missing limb was a testament to battles fought and survived. His left arm, the only one remaining, moved deftly as he adjusted the thick belt around his waist, the empty sleeve of his right arm tucked securely into it.

His coat, dark and salt-stained, swirled around his boots as he stepped forward, the weight of his presence almost palpable. There was a stiffness in his stride, not just from his wounds, but from the years of navigating turbulent waters and warring tides. His remaining eye, a steely, cold blue, scanned the gathered men, sharp with judgment and expectation. It was the kind of gaze that could either reassure a crew or make them quake in their boots.

Comerford's voice was deep and gravelly, carrying the wear of someone who had seen more than most. He spoke, his words blunt and without flourish, his Kilkenny accent thick but clear. "Right, lads. No time for coddlin'. We've a storm comin' and we need all hands on deck, wounded or not." There was an authority in his voice that left no room for questioning, a hardness borne from survival and the understanding of what it took to live another day on the sea. He was a captain, a survivor—one who knew that, in the world they lived in, mercy was often in short supply.

Captain Comerford

Marie Confides in Catherine

Marie sat by the hearth, nervously twisting a strand of her hair as the fire crackled softly. The warmth barely reached her, though she sat close enough to feel it. She stared into the flames, lost in thought. Outside, the sky was darkening, casting long shadows over the room. Catherine sat nearby, mending a tear in Ronan's shirt, the rhythmic sound of her needlework filling the silence.

Catherine glanced up, noticing the faraway look on Marie's face. "Marie? Ye've been quiet all day. Is something on yer mind?"

Marie hesitated, biting her lip. She had held onto her thoughts for days, too afraid to speak them aloud. But now, with the weight of her emotions pressing down, she couldn't keep them in any longer.

After a moment, she spoke softly. "Catherine… I think I'm falling in love with Rodrigo."

Catherine set her sewing aside, her surprise evident. "Rodrigo?" she asked, her voice a mix of curiosity and concern. "The Spaniard?"

Marie nodded, her heart pounding. "Aye. I know it sounds foolish, but I can't help how I feel. Every time I see him, I feel… something I've never felt before. Like there's a whole world outside of this one. A world where I could be more than just... this."

Catherine's expression softened as she leaned closer, placing a hand on Marie's arm. "It doesn't sound foolish at all. Rodrigo seems like a good man. And he's taken a shine to ye."

Marie's throat tightened as the fear she had been holding back spilled out. "But what if... what if he doesn't stay, Catherine? What if I'm just another person he meets before he sails away? I don't know what I'd do if I got my hopes up only to have him leave, or... or worse, realize I'm not enough for him."

Catherine's heart ached at the vulnerability in Marie's voice. She took Marie's hands in hers, giving them a reassuring squeeze. "Marie, listen to me," she said softly. "Rodrigo sees you. I've seen the way he looks at ye, like ye're the only thing that matters in the world. He cares for ye, I'm certain of it."

Marie looked up, her eyes glistening with unshed tears. "But what if I'm not enough? What if my illness holds him back? I'm not strong like ye or the others. I can't run through fields or sail on ships. He deserves someone who can live life with him, not someone who's always... weak."

Catherine's heart tightened as she heard the familiar doubt in Marie's voice. She had always feared that her frailty made her less. Catherine couldn't let her believe that anymore.

"Marie, ye are more than enough," Catherine said firmly, her eyes locking onto her sister's. "Yer illness doesn't define ye. It never has. Ye're kind, clever, and ye've a heart bigger than anyone I know. And Rodrigo? He's seen that. He doesn't care about how fast ye can run or how strong ye are. He sees you for who ye truly are."

Marie's lip trembled, but she shook her head. "But what if he leaves, Catherine? What if I hope for something that can never be?"

Catherine tightened her grip on her hands. "That's the risk, isn't it? But love is always a risk. It's never certain, but that doesn't mean it isn't worth it. Ye deserve happiness too. Ye deserve to love and be loved."

A tear slipped down Marie's cheek, and she quickly wiped it away. She wanted to believe Catherine's words, but the fear of being hurt still loomed large.

Catherine pulled her into a soft embrace. "Let yerself be loved, Marie. Ye've waited long enough."

Marie clung to her sister, feeling the comfort of her words sink in. For the first time, she allowed herself to imagine a future with Rodrigo—a future where she wasn't just the sickly girl, but a woman with someone by her side. The hope scared her, but it also filled her with warmth she hadn't known before.

As they pulled apart, Catherine gave her a soft smile. "Now, let's see how this unfolds. Ye may be surprised by how strong love can be, even when it's unexpected."

Marie nodded, a flicker of hope rising in her chest. For the first time, she began to believe that maybe—just maybe—Rodrigo might stay. And perhaps, she could be enough for him.

The Hunt and the Trial

Anna Island, Ballycroy

The next day dawned gray, the kind of overcast that weighed heavily over Black Sod Bay. Grace stood at the water's edge, watching as her men launched a small curragh. The boat bobbed on the choppy waters, heading toward the English warship anchored beyond the bay. Word had reached her overnight—five Spanish soldiers were hiding on Anna Island, a small outcrop barely three miles away. Bingham would not let this go unchecked.

By mid-morning, Bingham and Captain Todd Comerford had assembled a landing party. Their boat cut through the waves, heading directly for the island.

By afternoon, the soldiers were brought to Doona Castle—bound, beaten, and covered in mud, their faces gaunt from days of hiding. Alongside them was James McDoogle, the Irish farmer who had sheltered them. His hands were shackled, his face pale.

The grand hall of the castle was transformed into a makeshift courtroom. A swift military trial began, with Lord Bingham at the head of the table and Comerford standing by. The flickering torchlight cast long shadows, making the room feel smaller and more oppressive.

The Spanish soldiers, exhausted and fearful, were given no defense. One by one, they were condemned to death for treason. They stood silent, their fates sealed the moment they were captured.

James McDoogle was brought forward last. His voice trembled as he pleaded. "My lord, I didn't know they were hiding in my barn. I swear, I only found them two days ago. I'm innocent! I've a wife and three children—they need me!"

Bingham looked down at him, unmoved. "You housed traitors to the English Crown. You will hang for it."

McDoogle's knees buckled as the sentence crushed him. "No, please!" he screamed, tears streaming down his face. "My family—my children—what will they do without me?"

His cries echoed, but Bingham merely gestured to the soldiers. The verdict was final.

The Spanish Prisoners

The Hanging of the Soldiers

Fahy, Ballycroy

The next morning, the sky was a brilliant blue, a cruel contrast to the grim spectacle unfolding. The gallows had been hastily constructed outside the castle, with the sun gleaming on the Atlantic and the tide in, but all eyes were on the scaffold.

The condemned men were led out in chains, their heads bowed. A crowd had gathered—soldiers, villagers, even those who had helped rescue the Spanish survivors. Among them stood Daniel and Ronan, silent and grim. Marie watched from a distance, her face pale, heart heavy. Peggy, clinging to Nora's skirts, watched with wide, fearful eyes.

One by one, the Spanish soldiers were brought to the gallows. The first man went silently, his expression resigned. The rope was placed around his neck, the lever pulled, and his body dropped, hanging lifeless. The crowd murmured, but no one moved.

The second man, clutching a rosary, whispered a prayer as he met the same fate.

The third soldier, his eyes hollow, muttered incoherently in Spanish as he was led to the scaffold. His blank stare showed he had already given up.

Then came the fourth soldier, who broke the morning silence. "Por favor! I have a wife... children... please, do not hang me!" His voice trembled with terror as he fell to his knees, begging. "Mi familia… please!" His cries echoed, but Captain Comerford's cold stare hardened his men's resolve. They dragged him to the noose, and with a swift pull of the lever, his body dropped, and the cries stopped.

The fifth Spaniard went silently, composed, without a word.

The Prisoners Are Hanged

McDoogle

Finally, James McDoogle, the Irish farmer, was dragged to the scaffold. His face was a mask of terror, and tears streamed down his cheeks. "I didn't know! I swear to God I didn't know they were in my barn!" he pleaded, his voice hoarse. "Please, Lord Bingham, spare me! My family… please!"

The crowd shifted, murmurs rippling through the villagers who knew McDoogle. They doubted his guilt, but none dared speak against Bingham.

Bingham narrowed his eyes. "You harbored enemies of the Crown. For that, you will hang."

As the soldiers moved to tighten the noose, Grace O'Malley stepped forward, her voice clear and commanding. "Cut him down."

All eyes turned to her. For a moment, even the soldiers hesitated.

Bingham's gaze darkened. "What is the meaning of this, Grace? He's been sentenced."

Grace met his gaze without flinching. "McDoogle is innocent. He didn't know they were there. I know this man. He is no traitor."

Bingham's hand rested on his sword's pommel. "Aiding the Spanish is treason. Are you questioning my authority?"

"I am asking for mercy," Grace's eyes flashed with anger. "If you hang him, I will tell Queen Elizabeth you hanged an innocent man."

The tension between them crackled. After a long moment, Bingham's lips curled into a bitter smile. "Very well, Lady O'Malley," he said, sarcasm dripping from his voice. "Cut him down. But if I ever find him aiding the Spanish again, I will hang him and burn his farm."

Grace didn't blink. "He won't. You have my word."

The soldiers reluctantly untied McDoogle's hands, and he stumbled back into the crowd, still shaken but alive. The crowd murmured uneasily as Bingham turned away, announcing, "This matter is closed. Let it serve as a warning."

As the crowd dispersed, Grace stood firm, watching Bingham's retreating figure. This was only the beginning of the tension between them.

~ ~ ~ ~

From behind the crumbling stone wall of the stable, Marie and Rodrigo watched the grim spectacle unfold. The cold air clung to their skin, but neither felt it. Rodrigo leaned on his crutch, his face pale and tense, the pain in his wound nothing compared to the turmoil in his chest as he saw his fellow Spaniards dragged to their fate.

Marie stood beside him, hands clenched, her heart heavy. She watched as the men were led to the gallows, their faces etched with fear. The sound of the trapdoor echoed in the distance, sending a chill through her. One of the Spaniards pleaded for his life, his cries piercing the cold air. She closed her eyes, fighting back tears, her fingers brushing Rodrigo's arm in silent comfort.

Rodrigo's gaze was fixed on the gallows. "I could have been one of them," he murmured.

Marie turned to him, her heart aching. "But you're not," she whispered, tightening her grip on his sleeve. "You're here… and we will keep you safe."

They stood in silence as the final figure swung from the gallows. The crowd began to disperse, the tension still thick. Rodrigo lowered his head, pain flickering across his features. Marie rested her head on his arm, feeling both heavy and lighter knowing he was still alive.

Together, they remained hidden behind the wall, shielded from the cruelty of the world beyond.

Grace Stops McDoogle's Hanging

Rodrigo Tells Marie He is Staying

The next morning, the room was quiet, save for the distant wind howling outside. Marie sat on the edge of a small wooden bench, her hands tightly folded in her lap. Rodrigo stood across from her, his posture tense, as if sensing something heavy between them.

Marie had been struggling to find the right words. After the hangings of the men who tried to escape, her heart was filled with fear. She couldn't bear the thought of Rodrigo facing the same fate. But saying it aloud was harder than she imagined.

Finally, she spoke, her voice trembling. "Rodrigo, after what happened... I can't bear the thought of you being captured. If you stay, it could happen. I couldn't live with myself if something happened to you."

Rodrigo's brow furrowed as he stepped closer. "You want me to leave?" His voice was soft, but there was a tension behind his words.

Marie looked away, unable to meet his eyes. "You need to go, Rodrigo. You need to find your freedom. There's no safety for you here." She hesitated, her hands trembling. "I don't want to lose you."

Rodrigo was silent, his expression unreadable. Then, with care, he moved toward her, kneeling so their eyes met. "What would my freedom be without you?" he asked quietly, his voice filled with feeling.

Marie's heart skipped a beat. She looked at him, truly seeing him for the first time. The weight of his words sank in, and she realized how much she wanted him to stay, how much she had come to need him.

Rodrigo reached for her hand. "Marie, I'm falling in love with you. I know it's sudden, but I can't leave without you. You've become part of me."

Marie's breath hitched. She never imagined hearing such words from him. She opened her mouth, but he continued, his gaze steady.

"If I'm a danger to you, I'll leave," he said softly. "I can't bring harm to your family."

The silence that followed was thick with emotion. Marie felt a lump in her throat. She didn't want him to leave, but could she ask him to stay, knowing the risks?

Finally, she whispered, "You're not a danger now. No one knows you're here. Maybe… maybe you can stay."

Rodrigo's hand tightened around hers, hope flickering in his eyes. "Do you want me to stay?"

Marie nodded, tears threatening. "Yes. I don't want you to go. I've been so afraid of what might happen, but I don't want to lose you."

Rodrigo's smile softened, his determination clear. "Then I'll stay. With you."

Marie's chest tightened with relief. She didn't know what the future held, but in that moment, nothing else mattered. Rodrigo was staying. He had chosen her.

He pressed a soft kiss to her fingers. "We'll find a way through this. Together."

Marie smiled, her heart full. "Together," she echoed softly, holding on to the promise they had made.

At Elly Bay

The next night, after a tense journey, Don Alonso, Ronan, and their men reached Elly Bay. The darkness cloaked their movements as they scanned the area for signs of English forces. There were none. The tension was palpable, every man on alert for an ambush. A local villager, nervous but willing to help, informed them that an English ship, commanded by Captain Comerford, had been patrolling the coast.

"A Spanish ship was nearby," the villager whispered. "But it sailed north to avoid Comerford."

Ronan turned to Don Alonso. "We continue north. We stay hidden."

Don Alonso nodded. "Then north we go."

The day was spent hiding in dunes and rocks, every noise making the men flinch. As night fell, they moved again, silently like shadows. Approaching a nearby town, Ronan noticed the flicker of distant fires. He signaled for silence, hand on his sword, and he and Don Alonso, with trusted men, crept closer.

Ronan's heart leapt when he heard Spanish voices. They emerged from the shadows to find a camp of Spanish soldiers. In the harbor, a Spanish ship was undergoing repairs.

"Alonso!" A joyful voice called. From the fires, Captain Vasquez, an old friend of Don Alonso, strode forward with a broad smile. "I thought you were lost."

"Vasquez!" Don Alonso embraced his comrade. "It's a blessing to see you alive. What news?"

"We sail in six days," Vasquez said, gesturing to the ship. "The ship's being repaired. You and your men are welcome to stay."

Ronan, however, knew his journey wasn't over. His heart ached for home, for the warmth of his mother, the teasing of his sisters, and the comfort of Doona.

Later, Don Alonso and Captain Vasquez pulled Ronan aside. "You wish to return home, don't you?" Alonso asked kindly.

"Aye, Captain," Ronan admitted. "I've done what I came to do, but my family needs me."

Don Alonso placed a hand on Ronan's shoulder. "You've done more than anyone could ask. Captain Vasquez has arranged for a local man to take you by sea to Doona."

The next morning, as the sun rose, Ronan stood before Don Alonso. The captain's voice was steady but filled with warmth. "You're a brave young man, Ronan. You've saved my life twice. I admire you and count you as a friend."

Ronan swallowed, trying to suppress his emotions. "I learned a lot from you, Captain."

Don Alonso smiled faintly. "Not all men would have risen as you did. Perhaps someday, we'll meet again."

Ronan nodded. "I hope so, Captain."

Don Alonso handed Ronan a silver medallion, a token of gratitude. "Take this. You'll always have friends in Spain."

Ronan clutched the medallion, nodding silently. With a final farewell, he boarded the boat bound for home.

As the boat sailed away, the wind carried him back to Doona, his heart aching for his family, but swelling with pride for the journey he had taken. He was no longer the same boy who had left.

~ ~ ~ ~

Two days later, as Ronan approached the familiar landscape of Doona, his heart lifted. The village came into view, and there, standing near the gates, was Mary McBride. Her soft smile lit up her face as she spotted him. She stepped forward, her hands clasped tightly in front of her, as if nervous.

"I knew you'd make it back," Mary said, her voice soft but brimming with relief.

Ronan smiled, feeling something stir in his chest as he looked at her. She had grown even more beautiful in the days since he'd been away. "Aye, I'm back," he replied, the weight of his journey finally starting to lift.

Mary stepped forward and hugged him tightly. "Oh, I prayed for ye, Ronan. I prayed for ye."

In that moment, Ronan felt like he belonged, like she was his home. They pulled apart, but Ronan knew that the hug she had given him was a promise of life together someday.

The villagers gathered around as Ronan was welcomed back by his family. Nora wrapped her arms around him, tears in her eyes, and even little Peggy threw her arms around his waist. For a moment, the troubles of the world faded, and Ronan allowed himself to bask in the love and warmth of home.

The News

The next day, the door creaked open, and Daniel McManamon stepped inside, his face tight with worry. He glanced around, then motioned for Ronan and Nora with a sharp tilt of his head. "Come aside," he muttered, his voice low.

Ronan felt a knot in his stomach as he exchanged a glance with Nora. Together, they followed Daniel to the far side of the room.

"Bingham's men are comin' to search the village tomorrow," Daniel whispered urgently. "Flynn got word. We've little time."

Ronan's chest tightened. His thoughts immediately turned to Marie. She had recently confided in him about Rodrigo, her feelings stirring in a way they never had before. The thought of what this news would do to her—knowing they might have to send Rodrigo away—made his stomach churn.

"What are we going to do?" Nora whispered, fear in her eyes.

Daniel shook his head. "Rodrigo can't stay here. We'll have to move him, and soon."

Ronan's mind raced. "He's too weak," he said quietly, glancing down. "We need to bring Uncle Farrell in. He'll know what to do."

Nora nodded. "Aye, Farrell will have a plan."

As they turned back, Ronan's heart sank. Marie, usually so reserved, had overheard a flicker of the conversation. She looked up from her seat, her face pale, eyes wide with fear—not just from danger, but from the looming loss.

Her voice trembled as she approached. "Rodrigo... he has to go, doesn't he?"

Ronan didn't need to answer. She already knew.

Marie's face crumpled, and she clutched the edge of the table for support. The weight of it all—the chance she thought Heaven had granted her slipping away—pressed down on her. But even in her anguish, she forced herself to stand tall, nodding through her tears. "I know he must... but... I'll help," she whispered, her voice small but resolute.

Ronan placed a steady hand on her shoulder, his own heart breaking for her. Nothing was decided yet, but they all knew—Rodrigo couldn't stay, no matter the cost to Marie's fragile hope.

The Plan

The next day, the hearth crackled in the McManamon household, casting flickering shadows on the walls. Ronan stood in the corner, arms crossed, listening to his father Daniel, Farrell, and Nora. They spoke about the danger of Bingham's soldiers, the plan to move Rodrigo, and the risk of failure. But Ronan wasn't really hearing them. His thoughts churned restlessly beneath the surface.

For too long, he had been the boy in the background, always second in command. His father's stern guidance and Farrell's rough mentorship had never left space for Ronan to lead. When difficult decisions came, they never looked to him first. It felt as though they saw him as a child—unproven, uncertain.

But he wasn't a boy anymore.

Ronan's jaw tightened as his father spoke again, his words grating against Ronan's nerves. "Farrell will take Rodrigo," Daniel said. "It's too dangerous for anyone else."

Always Farrell. Always his father—never him. Ronan clenched his fists, nails digging into his palms. What had he done to make them think he couldn't handle this? He knew the coastline better than anyone. Yet they still treated him like a child in need of protection.

The fire crackled louder, filling the silence. Farrell nodded to accept the plan, but Ronan felt something burning inside him, hotter than the flames.

His father turned to him. "You'll stay here with the others, Ronan. Help your mother. Keep watch on the castle."

"No," Ronan said before he even realized it. His father and Farrell exchanged surprised glances.

"It should be me," Ronan continued, stepping forward. "I'll take Rodrigo."

His father opened his mouth to protest, but Ronan pressed on, his chest tightening with the need to be heard. "I know the coast better than anyone. I've done it before, and I can do it again. If anyone can get him safely to Geesala, it's me."

Daniel's face hardened, but Ronan met his gaze head-on. "You don't think I can handle it, do you?" he asked quietly, his voice carrying the weight of every moment he had been overlooked. "You think I'm still a boy."

His father hesitated. "It's not about that, Ronan. This is about the risk. You're not—"

"I'm ready," Ronan interrupted firmly. "You don't need to protect me anymore. I can do this."

Silence followed, the crackling fire the only sound. Ronan's heart pounded. This was his moment.

Farrell broke the silence with a slow nod. "He knows the way," he said, his voice supportive. "And he's right. He won't draw suspicion like I would."

Daniel exhaled, the tension easing slightly. "Alright," he said softly, though his reluctance remained. "But you be careful, Ronan. This isn't just about proving yourself."

Ronan nodded, heart still racing with both fear and exhilaration. "I'll bring him safely to the men," he said, his voice steady. He wasn't just doing this for his family—he was doing it for himself.

Marie Says Goodbye

Marie stood by the door, her hands tightly clasped as if to steady herself. Her face was pale, breath shallow, but beneath the trembling exterior was fierce determination. She knew this moment was coming, but that didn't make it easier.

Taking a deep breath, she stepped into the room where Rodrigo lay. His eyes were open, fixed on the ceiling, his brow furrowed with pain and sorrow.

"You have to go," she whispered, her voice fragile. She knelt beside him, her hand trembling on his arm.

Rodrigo turned his head slowly, his dark eyes meeting hers. "I know," he said, his voice low. "But leaving you... it's a wound deeper than any I've known."

Marie's chest tightened. She had spent weeks by his side, fighting for his survival. The thought of him leaving felt like being torn apart. "I love you, Rodrigo," she said, tears spilling over.

Rodrigo cupped her face gently, his thumb brushing away her tears. "I've grown to love you too," he whispered. "You gave me hope, but I cannot stay. If I stay, they will find me, and I will die." His thumb lingered on her cheek.

Marie shook her head, sobbing as she clutched his hand. "Then take me with you. Don't leave me here."

Rodrigo's heart broke at her words. "I must go so I can return. I promise I will come back. I will fight and survive—for you."

Her breath hitched as his words gave her a fragile sliver of hope. "Please, come back to me," she whispered.

Rodrigo, gritting his teeth against the pain, pulled himself up with his crutch. With great effort, he reached for her, pulling her close for a desperate, tender kiss.

"I swear, Marie," he murmured, "I will come back. No matter what it takes."

Tears streamed down her face as she clung to him. "I love you," she cried, her voice breaking.

Rodrigo held her close. "And I love you," he whispered. "But I must go."

He gently pulled away, their hands lingering for a moment before he hobbled toward the door. Marie's eyes followed him as he left.

As the door creaked shut, Marie sank to the floor, her hand pressed to her lips, still feeling the warmth of his kiss. Her heart swore it would wait for him, but her soul ached from the loss.

The Journey to the Sandy Banks

The night was moonless, dark sky pressing down as they moved along the cow path to the Sandy Banks. The soft shuffle of boots on dirt, the distant crash of waves—the only sounds breaking the silence. Behind them, the English soldiers' fires glowed faintly around the castle, like distant, ominous stars.

Farrell walked beside Ronan, clutching a small satchel, heavy with Spanish gold. "Once you reach Geesala, find Eamon. He'll have the cart ready," he muttered. "Be quick—the tide waits for no one."

Ronan nodded, his focus fixed ahead. The family followed—Nora, Daniel, Catherine, and Peggy, quiet and anxious, her usual spark dimmed.

They reached the shore, the sea stretching out dark and vast, the incoming tide lapping steadily. A small boat bobbed in the shallows, ready to take them across the inlet. Rodrigo leaned on Ronan, his face pale, breath shallow. There was no turning back.

Daniel gripped Ronan's shoulder. "This isn't easy, but I'm proud of you, son."

"I'll bring him safely, Da." Ronan met his father's eyes, feeling the weight of his words.

Farrell handed him the satchel and a pistol. "Keep your wits, lad. The night is your friend."

Nora pulled him into a fierce hug. "Come back to us, my boy."

"I will, Ma," he whispered.

Catherine hugged him, her face wet with tears, but Peggy clung to him the longest. "Don't let anything happen to you," she whispered fiercely.

"I won't, Peg." He ruffled her hair, smiling softly.

From the shadows, Mary McBride stepped forward. She wrapped her arms around him, then kissed him—quick, soft, full of meaning. For a moment, the weight of the night lifted.

A faint splash pulled Ronan back. He broke away, helping Rodrigo into the boat, then climbed in. "Let's go," he said, urgency in his voice.

Farrell and Daniel pushed them off, the oars dipping softly into the water. The boat moved swiftly into the inlet, the figures on shore fading into darkness. The flicker of distant fires dimmed on the horizon.

The sea was calm, but Ronan felt the weight of what lay ahead. They had a long journey before them. There would be no turning back now.

Rodrigo Loaded onto Boat

Where is Peggy

Nora and Daniel walked side by side, the cool night air wrapping around them as they made their way home. Behind them, Catherine walked with Mary McBride and her family, while Farrell and the others followed at a slow pace, their figures outlined by the distant glow of the English campfires near the castle.

When they reached the house, Catherine entered first, her face flushed from the walk. Nora stepped inside and sighed, letting her shawl fall from her shoulders. The tension of the night hung in the air, heavy and unspoken.

Nora glanced around, the usual noise of her children settling in for the night noticeably absent. She frowned, looking at Catherine, who was busying herself near the hearth.

"Where's Peggy?" Nora asked, suddenly aware of the silence.

Catherine turned, confusion crossing her face. "I thought she was with you," she replied, her voice tight.

Nora's heart skipped a beat, her eyes widening. "She's not with you?" she asked, panic creeping into her voice.

Catherine shook her head, the same fear sparking in her eyes. Nora's heart raced, her mind spinning as she looked around the room, desperate to see Peggy's familiar figure. Catherine, noticing the growing alarm on her mother's face, stepped forward.

"She was standing near the boat when we said goodbye," Catherine said quietly, her own fear rising as the realization began to sink in.

Daniel, who had been hanging his coat by the door, stopped mid-motion. His eyes met Nora's, wide with dread.

Nora's breath caught in her throat, and the full weight of the situation struck her. They both knew exactly what had happened.

"She's gone with Ronan," Daniel said, his voice thick with disbelief, a sinking feeling settling deep in his gut.

Nora's hand flew to her mouth as the truth crashed over them. Peggy had slipped away, determined and brave, following Ronan into the unknown.

~ ~ ~ ~

The rowboat scraped against the rocky shore of Geesala as Ronan jumped out, his muscles aching from the crossing. The tide was pulling out, and he barely made it ashore before the boat would be stranded. His breath came in shallow gasps as he hurried to help Rodrigo, pale and struggling to walk.

"Wait here," Ronan muttered, his voice tense. He quickly pulled the boat further up the shore and ran to secure a horse and cart, as planned.

The village was quiet, its cottages dark. With Farrell's gold in his pocket, Ronan found Eamon Munnelly, who agreed to provide him with a horse and cart after a brief, secret exchange. The horse snorted softly as Ronan urged it forward, the creaking wheels the only sound in the stillness.

Returning to the shore, Ronan hurriedly unhitched the horse and cart near Rodrigo, who was struggling with the pain in his leg. As Ronan pulled back the hay in the cart, a small figure stirred beneath it.

"What in...?" Ronan murmured, and then the figure moved again, making his heart stop.

"Peggy?" he hissed, pulling the hay back to reveal his sister, curled up and staring at him with wide eyes.

"Ye said I couldn't come," Peggy whispered, both fearful and determined. "But I came anyway."

Ronan stared, dumbfounded. His hands trembled, a mix of disbelief and frustration, but also admiration for her boldness. Still, this was no place for her.

"Peggy... you can't be here," he whispered urgently. "We're in the middle of—"

"There's no way back now," she interrupted, her voice trembling slightly but filled with resolve. "The tide's already out."

Ronan's heart sank. She was right—they couldn't go back.

Rodrigo, watching from the rocks, raised his head and gave a weary smile. "It seems your sister is braver than most."

Ronan shook his head. "Aye," he muttered, reaching down to help Peggy out of the cart. "You've gotten us into a mess, Peggy."

Despite his frustration, pride flickered in Ronan's eyes as he helped her to her feet. He placed her on the cart's seat next to him.

"There's no going back," he said to himself. "We move forward."

With one last glance at the receding sea, Ronan climbed onto the cart and urged the horse forward into the dark night. Their journey had just gotten more complicated—but they would face it together.

A Close Encounter

The road was a narrow, winding path, shadowed by hills and low stone walls. The cart creaked under the weight of hay and the hidden cargo beneath it. Ronan sat in the driver's seat, gripping the reins tightly, while Peggy crouched beside him, her small frame hidden by the piles of straw.

The night air was cold, biting against Ronan's face. He kept his eyes on the path ahead, his mind racing with the memory of what Farrell had said. The English were everywhere, their patrols scouring the countryside for Spanish survivors.

Rodrigo lay beneath the hay, his breathing shallow but steady. Ronan knew if they were stopped, there would be no way to explain the extra weight in the cart. His heart pounded, thoughts churning with what they would do if confronted.

As they approached a bend, the sound of boots and horses' hooves reached Ronan's ears. His breath caught. Soldiers. The cart rolled forward slowly, the squeak of its wooden wheels too loud in the stillness.

Peggy, sensing the tension, clutched the side of the cart, her wide eyes darting toward Ronan.

"We're coming up on them," Ronan muttered under his breath, gripping the reins tightly. "Stay quiet, and no matter what happens, let me do the talking."

Peggy nodded, sinking deeper into the cart, trying to disappear into the hay.

As they rounded the bend, Ronan's worst fears were confirmed. Four English soldiers stood in the road, their steel helmets glinting faintly in the moonlight. One stepped forward, raising his hand to halt the cart.

"Hold there!" the soldier barked, eyeing the cart with suspicion. "Where do ye think you're going with this load?"

Ronan swallowed, forcing himself to stay calm. "To Ballyshannon, sir. Bringing hay to my uncle's farm."

The soldier narrowed his eyes. "Ballyshannon, is it? Seems a bit late for hauling hay. What's your uncle's name?"

Ronan's mind raced. "Munnelly, sir. Eamon Munnelly. He's waiting for the hay before first light."

The soldier's gaze lingered on the cart a moment too long, suspicion flickering in his eyes. "We've orders to search every cart," he said, his tone hardening. "There's talk of Spanish survivors hiding in these parts."

Ronan's stomach churned. The soldiers shifted, one hand resting on a sword's hilt. Tension thickened in the air.

Just then, Peggy, scrunching her face in frustration, blurted, "Ah, c'mon now! Ye think we've got a whole Armada stuffed in here under hay?" She crossed her arms, glaring at the soldiers. "We've got a load of hay, no time for foolin'!"

The soldiers exchanged amused glances, chuckling at her boldness. The lead soldier waved them through with a dismissive motion. "On your way, then. Watch yourself on the road."

Ronan forced a smile, his heart pounding. "Thank you, sir," he said, clicking the reins and urging the horse forward.

As they passed, Peggy shot Ronan a sly smile. He shot her a warning look, his jaw tight, but deep down, relief flooded him.

They continued on the road, the soldiers' laughter fading behind them. Once they were far enough away, Ronan let out a shaky breath, loosening his grip on the reins.

"You could've gotten us killed," he muttered, though his words lacked bite.

Peggy grinned, mischief in her eyes. "Aye, but I didn't."

Ronan shook his head, a reluctant smile creeping onto his face. "You've got more nerve than sense."

They continued northward, the darkness closing in. The road to Ballyshannon stretched ahead, but Ronan knew the hardest part was yet to come. And he couldn't shake the feeling their luck was running out.

Soldiers Stop Them

A Narrow Escape

The sky had turned a murky gray as dusk settled over Ballyshannon, the air thick with tension. Ronan stood at the edge of the camp, his eyes locked on the horizon where the sea stretched dark and unforgiving before him. The salty wind whipped against his face as he felt the weight of the decision pressing down on him like a vise. The English forces were closing in—faster than anyone had expected. They were less than a mile away, and time was running out.

Behind him, Don Alonso and Captain Vasquez moved like men possessed, their voices low and urgent as they barked orders to the crew. The ship bobbed in the bay, ready to sail, but every second wasted was a step closer to capture. Fires flickered on the distant hills, the glow of the English encampments growing brighter as the evening shadows deepened.

Rodrigo had been helped onto the ship. Ronan and Peggy prepared to leave. Don Alonso stopped them. "No, Ronan. You can't go back. Look, they've seen you."

He pointed toward the hills, his hand trembling with intensity. Two English scouts sat on horseback, watching them like hawks.

"But we have to go!" Ronan said.

"You can't," Don Alonso exclaimed, "They'll kill you for aiding us."

Ronan's heart pounded in his chest as he turned back toward the camp. Men were scrambling, throwing supplies onto carts, loading the ship with frantic haste. He clutched the small stone cross Mary McBride had given him, uttering a quick prayer in his heart. He looked to Peggy standing near the cart, her wide eyes darting between him and the Spanish captains. He could see the fear in her face, the uncertainty. His stomach churned at the thought of leaving everything behind—his home, his family, his life. But there was no turning back now.

Don Alonso stepped closer, his face grim. "You must come with us now, or you'll be hung with the rest. There's no more time to decide."

Peggy, her voice trembling, looked up at Ronan. "You're taking him with you, aren't you?" she asked, her words filled with quiet desperation.

Don Alonso's gaze softened, but his urgency never wavered. "You're both coming. It's not safe for either of you here anymore."

Ronan's mind spun, thoughts crashing against the roar of the sea like waves on jagged rocks. His instincts screamed at him to stay, to fight, but the truth was staring him in the face. They couldn't fight—not here, not now. The English were too close. The flicker of torches in the distance became clearer, a line of soldiers marching toward them, ready to tighten the noose.

"We have to move *now*!" Captain Vasquez barked, his eyes scanning the coastline. "Those scouts will be riding back to their unit. If we're not on board before they return, we'll be overrun. The tide is turning, and if we don't sail within the hour, we're as good as dead."

Ronan's heart raced, his pulse pounding in his ears. He turned to Peggy, who reached for his hand, her small fingers gripping tightly, as though she could hold him here, keep him from making the choice that was already made. "We'll be alright, won't we?" she whispered, her voice barely audible over the rising wind.

Ronan forced himself to nod, though the fear gnawed at him, threatening to tear him apart. "Aye, Peg. We'll be alright."

Suddenly, a shout pierced the chaos. One of the lookouts on the outskirts of the camp sprinted toward them, his face pale with panic. "Soldiers! The English—they're less than half a mile away!"

The camp erupted into a storm of activity. Men shouted orders, rushing to gather provisions, weapons, anything they could carry. Captain Vasquez's voice thundered above the chaos, his commands sharp and unrelenting. "Get everything aboard! *Now!*"

Don Alonso grabbed Ronan's arm, his grip iron-tight, his voice low and urgent. "We leave now, or we're finished. If we're caught on land, it's over."

Ronan's stomach twisted as the weight of it all crashed down on him. He looked past the scrambling men and the rocking ship toward the horizon, where the English forces were creeping closer, torches flickering like the approach of death itself. They were too close. There wasn't enough time.

He turned back to Peggy, her wide eyes full of fear, and his heart broke. He had to get her out—*both* of them out—before it was too late. He took a deep breath, steadying himself, feeling the cold bite of the wind on his skin.

"Now, Ronan," Alonso urged, pulling him toward the boats.

Ronan hesitated only a second longer before he grabbed Peggy's hand and ran toward the water. There was no more room for doubt, no more time for fear. The tide was turning, and if they didn't sail soon, the English would be upon them.

The ship was their only chance. They had to get to sea—*now.*

At the Captain's Table

The lantern light flickered across the polished wood of the captain's table, casting a warm glow despite the creaking of the ship and the cold sea air seeping through the hull. Ronan sat across from Don Alonso, whose usually stern face softened with a fleeting smile. Beside Ronan, Peggy's wide eyes took in every detail—the silver goblets, the maps, the murmurs of the crew outside.

Captain Vasquez leaned back, his dark eyes studying Ronan. "So, this is the lad who braved the storm to pull our captain from the wreckage," he said, his voice laced with a smile. "Tell me, Alonso, is he as fearless as they say?"

Don Alonso nodded thoughtfully. "Brave enough to put many seasoned sailors to shame. He has the heart of a warrior."

Peggy grinned proudly. "He's the bravest there is."

Vasquez smiled but glanced at Ronan with a wistful look. "I have a son about your age," he said. "He dreams of battles and glory. I hope he becomes half the man you are."

Ronan shifted, feeling warmth from the praise he hadn't expected. Recent days had been full of storms, battles, and fear, but here, he felt something else—kinship. He straightened, meeting Vasquez's gaze with newfound confidence. "Thank ye, Captain. One day, I'll come to Spain and visit ye and your son. I'll ask Grace to bring me."

The room fell into a comfortable silence as Alonso and Vasquez exchanged a glance, their shared admiration for Ronan evident.

"Then it's settled," Don Alonso said, raising his goblet in a small toast. "To survival, kinship, and journeys yet to come."

Ronan and Peggy clinked their cups with the captains, and for that moment, the uncertainty of the sea and the threat of the English faded into warmth and shared hope.

Battle on the High Seas

North Atlantic, Tramore Beach in Donegal

The cold, salty air stung Ronan's face as he gripped the railing of the Spanish ship, staring into the endless stretch of darkening ocean. Two miles off the Irish coast, the ship cut through churning waters, but tension was suffocating. Ronan's heart pounded as unease settled in his chest. The stillness of the sea felt like a prelude to something terrible.

Beside him, Peggy stood close to Captain Don Alonso on the foredeck, her wide eyes taking in the vastness of the sea, clinging to Alonso's coat. Captain Vasquez paced the deck, eyes sharp, issuing commands to the crew.

Suddenly, a shout came from the crow's nest: "Sail on the horizon!" The call shattered the quiet. Ronan's heart leaped as he squinted at the dark silhouette, the British flag snapping in the wind.

"Comerford," Don Alonso muttered, his hand tightening around his sword. "Ready the men! To your stations!"

Chaos erupted as Vasquez's voice thundered, "Man the cannons! Prepare for battle!" The crew moved swiftly, loading cannons and securing the ship. Tension was thick—survival depended on speed and precision.

Ronan rushed to the cannon, his hands shaking as he loaded it with gunpowder and shot. He had never faced this, but there was no time for hesitation.

On the foredeck, Peggy clung to Alonso's side, dwarfed by the chaos. Alonso's protective hand rested on her shoulder, eyes fixed on the enemy ship. "Stay close, lass," he murmured, though his gaze never wavered.

The British ship drew closer, its cannons gleaming ominously. Ronan's chest tightened. "Fire!" Don Alonso roared, and the ship shuddered as the cannons exploded to life, deafening the air.

The first volley missed, but the second struck, splintering the British hull with a satisfying crack. The British ship returned fire, and cannonballs tore through the air, sending debris and splinters flying.

"Reload!" Vasquez shouted, his face streaked with blood. Ronan gritted his teeth, sweating as he worked to reload under the pounding barrage.

The British ship pressed the attack, firing relentlessly. The Spanish ship rocked under each blast. Fire began to lick at the wood, smoke billowing across the deck, making it hard to breathe, see.

A blast shook the deck near Ronan, throwing him off his feet. He slammed into the railing, disoriented, blood pooling beneath him. Pain radiated through his side. Gasping, he forced himself up, struggling against the pain to reach the cannon rope.

A shadow loomed over him—an English sailor with his sword raised high. Before Ronan could react, a blast of gunfire stopped the man mid-stride. Ronan turned to see Don Alonso, his smoking pistol raised.

"Stay alive, lad!" Alonso shouted, his voice fierce, before turning back to the fight.

The battle raged on. The Spanish ship was taking heavy damage, its sails torn, flames spreading across the deck. Vasquez's face was grim. "We can't take much more of this!" he shouted, blood running down his arm. "Prepare to abandon ship!"

The crew scrambled to lower lifeboats as flames roared higher. Suddenly, a deafening roar split the air as a cannonball tore through the side of the ship. The deck trembled violently, and the acrid smell of gunpowder thickened. Bodies were thrown into the sea by the impact. Alonso, standing firm, was thrown back by the blast, blood soaking through his uniform as he clutched his side.

Just when all seemed lost, a thunderous boom echoed across the water. Another ship entered the fray, cannons blazing. The O'Malley flag flew high above its masts, and hope surged through the Spanish crew.

"Grace," Ronan whispered, his heart pounding.

Grace O'Malley's ship stormed into the battle, firing with deadly precision. Comerford's men scrambled to return fire, but Grace's ship moved too fast. Each cannon volley ripped through the British hull, sending flames into the air.

The tide had turned.

The Spanish crew, now with renewed hope, scrambled to abandon their sinking ship. Ronan grabbed Peggy and pulled her toward the side. "We have to go! Now!"

Together, they jumped into a lifeboat, cold seawater splashing against them. Around them, Grace's crew pulled Spanish sailors from the water, the O'Malley ship towering over the wreckage.

But as they looked around, there was no sign of Rodrigo.

"Ronan!" Peggy's voice cracked with panic. "Where's Rodrigo?"

Ronan's heart clenched. He searched the water, the wreckage, but Rodrigo was gone.

The battle was over. Comerford's ship was sinking, flames consuming it, while Grace's ship roared one last time to finish the job. But for Ronan, the victory felt hollow. Rodrigo was gone.

As Grace's ship pulled alongside them, her men hauled Ronan and Peggy aboard. Ronan collapsed, gasping for breath, Peggy clinging to his side. Grace O'Malley stood above them, her red hair wild in the wind. "You fought well, lad," she said, her voice steady, "But not all battles end in victory."

Ronan nodded weakly, exhausted, his heart heavy with loss. They had survived—but not everyone had.

Duquesa Santa Ana Under Attack from Comerford

Rodrigo is Lost

The wreckage of the battle smoldered on the horizon, flames licking the night sky as Grace O'Malley's ship sailed to rescue the survivors. Ronan and Peggy clung to each other in the lifeboat, their faces pale with exhaustion and fear. Around them, the sea was a graveyard of shattered masts and floating bodies, the remnants of the Spanish ship and Comerford's vessel.

Grace's ship brought hope, but Ronan's heart pounded with dread. "Rodrigo," he whispered, his voice hoarse from smoke and strain. His eyes searched the water, scanning every shadow and broken mast. "Peggy, where is he?"

Peggy's breath hitched, her knuckles white as she gripped the boat. "I saw him," she whispered, trembling. "Before the ship went under, I saw him."

Ronan's chest tightened. Rodrigo had been beside him moments before. He could still hear his voice, but now... now, he was gone.

The lifeboat rocked with the waves as Ronan stood, desperate. "Rodrigo!" he shouted, his voice raw. "Rodrigo!"

There was no answer.

Peggy's wide, terrified eyes met his. "Where is he, Ronan? We can't leave him." Her voice cracked under the weight of her fear.

Ronan turned back to the sea, his heart racing. Survivors clung to debris, but Rodrigo was not among them. "Pull up alongside them!" Ronan shouted to Grace's crew. "There are more out there!"

"The current's too strong," a sailor called back. "Anyone still out there..."

Ronan refused to believe it. He leaned over the side, scanning every inch of the dark water. "Rodrigo!" he cried, the name tearing from his throat. Memories of their friendship flashed through his mind. He couldn't be gone. Not Rodrigo.

Peggy's trembling hand reached his arm. "He has to be out there," she whispered, tears filling her eyes. "I promised Marie I'd bring him home."

Ronan's heart clenched. He couldn't face Marie without Rodrigo. The hope in her eyes when they left—he couldn't take that from her.

"Lad, the ship's going down," a sailor warned, glancing nervously at the sinking wreckage. "If he's not found soon, it'll be too late."

Grace O'Malley herself came down to pull Ronan back onto the ship's deck. Her battle-worn face softened as she looked at him. "There's nothing more ye can do, boy," she said quietly. "The sea's taken him."

Ronan shook his head, his throat tight. "I won't leave him."

But even as he spoke, he knew deep down that Rodrigo was gone.

The lifeboat drifted from the wreckage as Grace's crew pulled survivors aboard. Ronan collapsed back into the boat, Peggy beside him, her tears falling freely.

"Marie," Peggy whispered, clutching the hem of Ronan's coat. "How will we tell her?"

Ronan's chest ached, the bond with Rodrigo weighing on him like a ghost. He closed his eyes, fighting back tears. He had led Rodrigo to this fate, and now, in the cold aftermath of battle, the loss was unbearable.

Grace's ship hauled them aboard, drenched and hollow. On the deck, Ronan and Peggy watched the sea swallow the last of the wreckage.

But Rodrigo was gone.

A New Beginning

The moon hung low over Black Sod Bay, its pale glow casting silver ripples across the water. Grace O'Malley's ship slipped silently into the bay, its sails drawn, the oarsmen rowing in a quiet, steady rhythm. The dark silhouette of Slieve Mor loomed against the sky, the castle and village still and unaware of the new arrivals.

Ronan stood at the bow, his eyes fixed on the familiar shore growing closer with every pull of the oars. He turned to Peggy, huddled against him, her eyes wide with anticipation and exhaustion. As the ship touched land, Ronan felt his heart swell. Home. They had made it.

Before anyone else could move, Ronan knelt by Peggy, his voice low, careful not to wake those resting below deck. "Peggy," he whispered, "before we head home, there's somewhere I need to go. Will ye come with me?"

Peggy blinked, curiosity in her tired eyes, but she nodded. "Aye, Ronan. I'll go with ye."

They slipped off the ship, their feet finding the soft earth of the shore. With careful steps, they made their way up the winding path toward the village. The moonlight lit their way over hills and fields. The village was silent, dark windows watching as they passed.

Ronan's heart pounded as they approached a familiar cottage. The McBride's place stood at the end of the lane, its thatched roof glowing faintly under the moon. He paused outside the gate, looking down at Peggy.

"Ye ready?" he whispered, a small smile tugging at his lips. Peggy, her eyes bright with excitement, nodded.

Ronan drew in a deep breath, then pushed open the gate, its hinges creaking softly. He made his way to the door, his heart hammering as he raised his hand to knock.

A moment later, the door opened, and Mary McBride stood there, her eyes widening in surprise. She looked from Ronan to Peggy, her face a mix of confusion and hope.

"Ronan?" she whispered.

Ronan smiled nervously, rubbing the back of his neck. "Mary... I know it's late, but I've got somethin' to ask ye." He glanced at Peggy, who beamed at Mary.

Mary blinked, stepping back, her eyes never leaving Ronan. "What is it?"

Ronan stepped closer, his eyes locking onto hers. He reached for her hand, his fingers curling around hers gently. "Mary McBride... will ye marry me?"

For a moment, Mary just stared, her mouth opening in a silent gasp. Tears filled her eyes, and she nodded, a smile spreading across her face. "Aye, Ronan," she whispered, her voice breaking. "Aye, I will."

Peggy clapped her hands, her face glowing with happiness. Ronan pulled Mary into a tight hug, relief washing over him like a wave. He had faced storms and danger, but this was the moment he feared most. And she had said yes.

They pulled apart, Mary's eyes shimmering with tears, her hand gripping Ronan's tightly. "We have to go now," Ronan said softly. "Me ma and da will be worried sick about Peggy. I'll come back in the mornin'."

Mary nodded, her smile never faltering. "Go on then, Ronan. I'll be here."

Ronan squeezed her hand one last time, then turned to Peggy, who gave Mary a quick hug before taking her brother's hand. They stepped back into the night, the gate closing softly behind them.

Hand in hand, they set off down the lane, the moon lighting their way as they headed home—together.

Ronan and Peggy Come Home

The fire crackled softly in the hearth, casting a warm glow across the room. Marie sat by the window, her fingers wrapped around a piece of embroidery, though her eyes barely saw it. Beside her, Catherine rested her head on Marie's shoulder, the two sisters silent, lost in their own thoughts. Nora sat nearby, her gaze fixed on the flames as if in prayer.

A sudden noise broke the stillness. A voice, calling from outside, familiar yet almost unbelievable. "Mam! Da! It's me!"

Nora's head snapped up, her eyes widening. Marie and Catherine exchanged a look, the embroidery dropping from Marie's hands as they rushed to their feet.

"Ronan!" Marie whispered, her breath catching.

The door burst open, and his voice called again. "Mam! Peggy's here too!"

The room erupted into movement. Marie and Catherine bolted outside into the twilight, their eyes widening as they saw their brother standing there, his face flushed from the cold, Peggy just behind him, her eyes shining.

"Ronan!" Catherine called, her voice breaking as she reached out.

Before he could react, his sisters wrapped their arms around him, holding him tight. Peggy was enveloped too, her small frame barely visible in the tangle of arms.

Nora stood frozen for a moment at the door, her eyes locked on her children. Tears brimmed and spilled over as she dropped to her knees, sobbing with relief. She had feared the worst, spent each night praying for their safety, and now they were home, whole and unharmed.

"Thank you, God," she whispered, her voice cracking.

Daniel appeared at the doorway, his face etched with disbelief and joy. He bent down, wrapping his arms around Nora and lifting her gently to her feet. "They're back, love," he whispered, his voice thick with emotion. "They're home."

He guided Nora toward their children, who turned to see their mother, her face streaked with tears of joy. The family moved together, an embrace of love and gratitude, holding each other as if afraid they might disappear.

After what felt like a lifetime, Daniel's voice broke through the moment. "Come now, come inside," he said, his arm around Ronan's shoulders, his other hand resting on Peggy's head. "Let's get you all warm by the fire."

Together, they made their way inside, the door closing behind them, shutting out the cold night. The warmth of the hearth welcomed them, the flickering flames casting a golden light across their faces as they settled around it.

Nora knelt by the fire, cupping Ronan's face as she looked at him, her eyes taking in every detail, as if to reassure herself he was truly there. "My boy," she whispered, her voice breaking, "my brave boy."

Peggy sat on Daniel's knee, her small fingers reaching toward the fire, her wide eyes still shining. Marie and Catherine huddled close to Ronan, their laughter mingling with tears, relief washing over them in waves.

Daniel stood behind them all, his heart swelling as he looked at his family, finally whole again. He closed his eyes for a moment, breathing in the warmth, the love, the sound of their voices filling the room.

"What happened out there?" Daniel asked, his voice a low rumble as he stepped forward, his eyes scanning Peggy for more than just a physical report.

Peggy took a deep breath, the images of the battle fresh in her mind. "We were sailin' south, near Ross Point, and we saw an English ship…" She paused, her eyes flickering with the memory of cannons firing, the sea roaring, and the chaos of battle. "It was Comerford."

Nora gasped softly, her hand flying to her chest. "Comerford? The English captain?"

Peggy nodded, her face tightening. "Aye. His ship came at us fast. Don Alonso and Captain Vasquez were shoutin' orders, the men runnin' to the cannons. We fought, Ma… we fought hard, but…" Her voice wavered, and her hands began to tremble. "The ship… it started to sink. Fire everywhere."

Marie's eyes grew wide as she gripped the arm of her chair, leaning closer. "What about Rodrigo?" she asked, her voice almost pleading. The color drained from her face.

Peggy's face dropped, and the room seemed to grow colder. Her hands clenched into fists, her gaze falling. "We didn't find him," she said quietly, the words like a stone dropping into a well of silence.

Marie's breath caught in her throat, her heart twisting painfully. She stood abruptly, her chair scraping against the stone floor. "No… no, that can't be…" She took a step toward Peggy, her eyes wild with disbelief. "He was with ye. He… he has to be alive. He promised!"

Peggy shook her head slowly, tears welling in her eyes. "We looked, Marie. Grace's ship came, and we searched. But… but we couldn't find him."

A strangled sob escaped Marie, and she turned, running out of the house into the twilight, the door slamming behind her. The cold air hit her face as tears streamed down her cheeks, her heart shattering with each step. She collapsed near the stone wall by the stable, burying her face in her hands, her body trembling with grief.

Nora moved to follow, but Daniel placed a hand on her arm, gently stopping her. "Let her be," he whispered. "She needs time."

Peggy stood frozen in the doorway, guilt and sorrow weighing heavy on her small shoulders. "I'm sorry, Ma. I… I didn't mean for this."

Nora crossed the room, kneeling in front of Peggy, her hands cupping her daughter's tear-streaked face. "It's not your fault, Peggy. Ye did all ye could. You're a brave girl, and ye came home." She kissed her forehead, pulling her into a gentle embrace.

Daniel, standing nearby, looked out the door toward where Marie had run, his face dark with sorrow. "She'll heal," he said quietly. "But it'll take time."

The wind howled softly outside, carrying the bitter sting of loss, yet through it all, there was a flicker of hope. They were home—alive, together, and that alone was something to hold on to, even in the darkest moments.

Peggy, still wrapped in her mother's arms, whispered softly, "I hope he comes back, Ma… I hope he does."

Nora's gaze followed Marie's path out the door, her heart heavy with worry for both of her daughters. "So do I, Peggy," she said quietly, "so do I."

The Wedding

Fahy Church, Ballycroy

The following week, the air in Doona was filled with the sounds of celebration. The old Fahy Church grounds were alive with people—family, friends, and villagers who had gathered to witness the marriage of Ronan McManamon and Mary McBride. The old stone walls of the church stood proudly in the background as the local priest, Father Chris, prepared to bless the union.

Grace O'Malley stood among the crowd, her imposing figure a mix of elegance and strength. Her red hair, caught in the wind, danced like fire, and her eyes glinted with approval as she watched the young couple take their vows.

Uncle Farrell stood by Ronan's side, his broad grin revealing his pride in the boy he had helped raise. When the moment came, he stepped forward and handed Ronan a small pouch. "Ten pieces of Spanish gold," he said, his voice low but warm. "May it bring ye luck."

Ronan smiled, his heart full as he accepted the gift. "Thank ye, Uncle."

Daniel, Ronan's father, placed a hand on his son's shoulder. "I'm givin' ye the three fields by the shore," he said, his voice thick with emotion. "They'll be yer start."

Ronan nodded, his throat tight with gratitude. "I'll make ye proud, Da."

As the priest concluded the ceremony, Mary's hand in Ronan's tightened, and the crowd erupted into applause. The village of Doona had turned out in full, their faces alight with joy at the sight of the young couple beginning their life together.

Ronan kissed his new wife, his heart nearly bursting with happiness. The Atlantic winds swept over the castle, carrying with it the promise of a new chapter, a new journey, and the hope that love—despite the battles and hardships—would always endure.

And as the sun set on that glorious day, the future of Ronan and Mary McManamon stretched out before them, filled with possibility and the promise of a life well-lived together.

Ronan and Mary's Wedding at Fahy Church

Marie Stares out to Sea

The sky was a brilliant blue the day Marie finally left her room. The grief had weighed her down like a leaden blanket, and for days she couldn't bring herself to move, let alone face the world. But something had shifted inside her, a slow but steady realization.

She walked along the cliffside where she had last seen Rodrigo, the wind tugging at her hair. For the first time in weeks, she let herself think of him, not with sorrow, but with gratitude. She stopped by the edge of the cliffs, her eyes scanning the horizon where Rodrigo's ship had disappeared. He was gone, but the love they had shared… that remained.

"I loved him," she whispered to the wind, her voice soft but sure. "And he loved me." For the first time, the weight in her chest lifted slightly, replaced by a deep, unshakable truth.

Her hands clasped the small stone cross Rodrigo had left with her, its rough edges familiar and comforting. "I'm not the same woman I was," she said aloud, her voice stronger now. "Loving him has changed me, and I'm stronger for it. I'm worthy of the love we shared." A tear slipped down her cheek, but it wasn't from grief. It was from acceptance. "I've loved. I've lived. And I was worthy of it all."

As she stood there, staring out at the endless horizon, she felt a quiet peace settle over her heart. She knew Rodrigo would never return, but he had left her with something more powerful than his presence—he had left her with a belief in herself. She had found strength in their love, and that strength would carry her forward.

The Girona

The wind howled off the coast, salt air stinging the gathered men. Captain Fabricio Spinola stood tall, his officers clustered around him, their faces grim. The last rays of the setting sun cast an orange glow across the rocky shore. Behind them, the Girona rocked gently, her weathered sails barely moving.

Don Alonso sat on a rough wooden chair, his leg bandaged, his face pale but his eyes burning. Pain etched every movement, but his voice held authority.

"We cannot be wrecked on Ireland again, Don Alonso," Spinola said firmly. "The English control the coast south of here. We're safer in Scotland."

Don Alonso gripped the armrests, his knuckles white. "I should take charge of the Girona," he demanded, his voice strained.

"You cannot," Spinola snapped. "You're badly injured. We cannot risk a captain who can barely stand."

Don Alonso's frustration flared, but he nodded, his body slumping. Only the waves filled the silence, crashing against the rocks.

"It is too dangerous to sail north," Alonso argued, wincing with every breath. "Grace O'Malley can aid us. I know where to find harbor."

"No," Spinola said sharply. "We sail north and around Ireland. It's not worth the risk."

Tension thickened the air. Spinola's voice cut through it. "We cannot take all of your men. There's not enough room on the Girona."

Don Alonso lurched to his feet, pain etched on his face, his voice raw. "You must take all of us! Any man left behind will be slaughtered. The English are closing in."

Spinola glanced at the dying light on the horizon. "Very well. Assemble everyone on the shore. No one brings anything extra. We sail with only five days' provisions."

The wind whipped through them as orders were given. Don Alonso lowered himself back into the chair, trembling with pain. His officers hovered, their loyalty clear, helplessness heavy.

"No torches or fires after dusk," Spinola commanded. "As soon as we're loaded, we sail."

"Sail tonight," Alonso urged, urgency in his voice.

"Yes," Spinola nodded, meeting his eyes. "Tonight."

The sea roared louder, a fitting answer to their fate. The men scattered to carry out the orders. Don Alonso stared at the dark water, knowing the northern route was dangerous. But there was no choice left. The Girona would sail, and the sea would decide their fate.

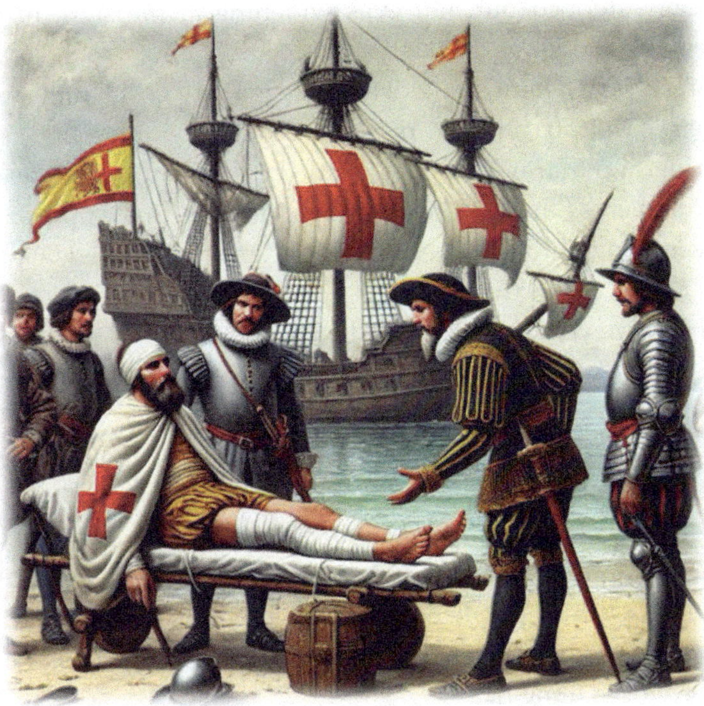

Don Alonso Pleads with Captain Spinola

Grace Rides Out

One week later.

Grace O'Malley rode out from her castle, tall and imposing atop a black horse. Her pirate's attire glinted under the pale sun, a red ribbon tied in her reddish-gray hair. She moved with purpose, her officers, Flynn and Flaherty, flanking her as they descended the narrow path toward Daniel McManamon's cottage. The thudding of hooves broke the silence, carried by the sweeping wind.

When they reached the cottage, Grace reined in her horse and glanced at the weathered home. Daniel emerged, wiping his hands on his trousers, curiosity etched on his face.

"Is Ronan here?" Grace's voice was steady, though her eyes carried unspoken weight.

Daniel nodded. "Peggy, go fetch Ronan," he said quietly.

Peggy stepped out, her eyes widening at the sight of Grace. She curtsied, awe in her gaze. "Hello, Grace."

Grace gave a faint smile. "Hello, Peggy, my girl. Hurry now."

Peggy ran off, and the rest of the family gathered outside—Nora, Catherine, and Marie. A stillness settled over them as they waited.

From across the field, Ronan and Mary McBride approached, their figures cutting through the tall grass. As they neared, Grace offered Ronan a long, respectful nod.

"How are ye, Ronan?" she asked softly.

"I'm good, Grace," he replied, tilting his head. "Ye look grand on that horse."

She nodded tightly, her voice grave. "I've just had word from Sorley Boy MacDonnell, the chieftain in Donegal."

The others leaned in, tension thick in the air.

"Don Alonso and his men," Grace continued, her eyes hardening, "they boarded a ship called The Girona, bound for Scotland. But they didn't make it. They were wrecked on the rocks at Lacanda Point."

The words hung heavy.

"Thirteen hundred souls aboard," she added softly, sorrow threading her voice.

Ronan's face twisted in disbelief. "Thirteen hundred? How could there be so many?"

Grace met his gaze, compassion softening her weathered face. "Ye'll learn, Ronan. At sea, desperation drives hard choices."

Daniel's voice was hushed. "Were there any survivors?"

Grace shook her head, her lips pressed tight. "A small handful. Less than ten."

The silence was suffocating. Ronan stood motionless, fists clenched, while Marie's hand found his, offering silent comfort.

Grace surveyed the gathering, her heart heavy with the weight of their grief. Meeting Ronan's eyes one last time, she gave a nod of solidarity before turning her horse. The officers followed, their hooves fading into the distance, leaving the McManamons in stillness and sorrow.

Grace Delivers the News

On the Girona

The wind howled like a wounded beast. Black clouds churned in the sky, blotting out the stars. The waves were monstrous, crashing against the deck like the fists of an angry god. The Girona pitched and groaned, its timbers straining under the rage of the sea.

Rodrigo clung to the railing, salt spray soaking his face, his hair whipped by the gale. He had survived the Duquena Santa Ana, but tonight fate felt less merciful. Whispering a prayer his mother had taught him, he fought to hold on against the storm's fury.

Don Alonso winced, leaning against the mast, his wounded leg barely supporting him. Each step was agony. He knew he would never leave Ireland alive, never see Spain or his family again. His heart twisted as he prayed for his wife and children, for their safety, for their forgiveness.

A voice cracked through the storm. "Rocks!"

Panic erupted. Men screamed and scrambled, slipping on rain-slicked boards, their faces contorted with terror. The Girona lurched violently, the hull grinding against unseen stone. Rodrigo's chest tightened as the ship shuddered, splintering wood groaning under the assault. The ship's belly was being torn apart.

A deafening crash silenced the prayers and cries. Rodrigo was thrown to the deck, the impact stealing his breath. The Girona split with a thunderous crack, leaving an eerie, fleeting quiet before chaos consumed the night.

The sea rushed in, devouring the broken ship. Rodrigo heard men's screams, their desperate cries rising above the storm. They clung to ropes, to wreckage, to each other, but the waves were merciless, tearing them from their hold. Bodies tumbled, limbs flailed, faces twisted in terror as the icy water dragged them into its depths.

Rodrigo struggled to stay afloat, the cold pulling at him, his chest burning. Around him, voices pleaded with heaven, but the storm offered no mercy. The Girona was gone, its men claimed by the sea.

Don Alonso, eyes closed, whispered a final prayer as the deck gave way beneath him. He plunged into the darkness, the cries of his men a haunting symphony of despair.

The jagged rocks loomed in the shadows, unyielding against the waves. The sea swallowed the ship piece by piece until nothing remained but shattered debris, drifting in the endless, uncaring ocean.

The Girona Hits the Lacanda Point Rock

At the Sandy Banks

Marie stood still, her breath catching in her throat, eyes narrowing at the distant figure stumbling over the sand dunes. The wind gusted off Black Sod Bay, carrying a salty chill and tugging strands of hair loose from her braid. Her heart raced as the figure grew closer, but her mind resisted, unwilling to accept the impossible.

Could it be him?

The sun fought to pierce the gray clouds clinging to Slieve Mor, casting thin beams of light onto the shore. The scene looked almost dreamlike. The cows moved lazily ahead, oblivious to the shift in the air.

But Marie's world had stopped. Her pulse quickened, unsure if her eyes were playing tricks.

For weeks, rumors had reached Doona—bodies washing ashore, ships lost, men drowned. And Rodrigo… no one had seen him since that night. Hope had dwindled with each passing day, but Marie refused to surrender completely, clinging to the smallest sliver of faith.

Now, this figure.

She dropped the stick in her hand, her legs frozen as the figure disappeared into a dip between the dunes, only to rise again.

"Rodrigo!" The name tore from her lips, carried by the wind but barely audible above the sea's roar.

She had imagined this moment too many times, only to wake to cold reality. Her heart had been bruised by hope before. But this felt different.

She took a tentative step forward, then another, her feet quickening as the figure reached the final dune, stumbling, waving an arm. Her heart stuttered.

"Rodrigo!" she screamed, her voice cracking with raw desperation.

The figure stopped, waving both arms now. She saw him clearly. His clothes were ragged, torn from the journey. His once-strong frame moved with a pronounced limp, but it was him—alive, breathing, here.

Marie's legs obeyed, and she took off running. The cows scattered as she sprinted, the wind whipping her face. Each step carried her faster, fueled by disbelief and hope. The dunes stretched on forever, but none of it mattered.

"Rodrigo!" she cried again, tears streaming, her voice breaking.

She closed the distance, her feet pounding the earth. Every second felt like eternity. She feared he might vanish, but he was real. He was here.

Rodrigo reached the bottom of the dune, his movements labored. When their eyes met, everything else melted away—the pain, the fear, the agonizing wait. They ran toward each other, their steps uneven, their hearts desperate to reunite. When they collided, Marie threw herself into his arms, clinging tightly. She sobbed into his chest, her tears soaking his torn shirt.

"You're alive! Rodrigo, you're alive!" Her voice cracked with joy and disbelief, her fingers gripping him as if afraid he might slip away.

Rodrigo's arms wrapped around her, trembling. "I told you, Marie," he whispered, his voice thick with emotion. "I promised I'd come back to you."

Marie pulled back just enough to see his face. He was thinner, worn by the sea and journey, but alive.

"I thought…" she began, but her voice faltered.

"I love you, Marie," Rodrigo said softly, his voice raw. "I've thought of nothing but getting back to you."

"I love you too," she sobbed. "I thought I'd lost you."

Rodrigo cupped her face, brushing away her tears. "I fought to survive—for you. Every wave, every step, it was for you."

They kissed, the world fading into the sound of their breath and hearts. The sea roared, but it no longer felt menacing.

Marie clung to him, unable to stop the tears. He was solid, real. He had survived the impossible and come back to her.

"You're home," she whispered, her voice full of awe and joy. "You're really home."

Rodrigo, pressing his forehead to hers. "And I'll never leave again."

Rodrigo Returns to Marie

Rodrigo's Account

Rodrigo sat before Grace, Flynn, Flaherty, Daniel, and Ronan, his face drawn and pale, the horrors of his experience still etched in his eyes. The fire crackled softly, the only sound in the tense silence as the others leaned forward, hanging on his every word. His voice, rough and broken from exhaustion, filled the room, carrying the weight of his ordeal.

"On the *Duquesa Santa Ana,* two other sailors and myself were thrown into the sea during the battle. We managed to grab hold of a piece of wood—just enough to keep us afloat—and tried to swim out of the range of the fighting. The cannon fire, the smoke, the screams—they were all around us. But somehow, we made it to shore."

Rodrigo paused, his hands shaking slightly as he rubbed them together, trying to steady his nerves. His eyes flicked toward Grace, and then back down at his hands as he continued.

"We saw it. We saw Grace O'Malley's ship—*your* ship—sink Blakemore's warship. I'll never forget that sight." His voice quivered with awe. "We saw their boats... blown apart by your cannons, Grace. The English never stood a chance. As the survivors from Blakemore's crew tried to row toward shore, we watched your men blow them out of the water."

Grace's gaze remained fixed on him, her expression unreadable, but there was a flicker of something—perhaps recognition of the brutal reality of her command.

"We were there," Rodrigo continued, "on the beach, to greet the first survivors who made it ashore. Don Alonso... he was among them. He was badly injured, barely conscious. We had to carry him from the water. Some English soldiers made it to shore, too, but... our men dealt with them. We couldn't afford to let any of them escape. If they'd made it back to warn the English soldiers inland, we'd have been wiped out before we even had a chance to rest."

There was a grim nod from Flynn, a silent acknowledgment of the necessity of the brutal decision.

Rodrigo swallowed hard, his voice lowering. "We camped for the night, but it was only a brief respite. Word came by morning—a Spanish galleon, the *Girona,* was moored for repairs just six miles away, at a place called Killybegs Harbor. We had no choice but to move immediately. We carried our wounded, including Don Alonso, and trekked through the night to reach Killybegs."

His face darkened as he recounted the events that followed. "When we got there, I saw Don Alonso and the captain of the *Girona*, Fabricio Spinola, arguing. I don't know what it was about, but they were pointing in different directions—both desperate, I suppose, to save their men. In the end, Spinola won the argument, and we were allowed to board. But the ship... it was already too crowded. There were nearly 1300 souls packed onto that galleon. I feared for my life, I won't lie. Something deep inside me told me not to board."

He hesitated, his voice faltering as a wave of guilt washed over him. "But to refuse would've been treason. And we all knew what that meant. Three men from our company tried to escape, tried to avoid boarding. They were caught... and hung in the harbor as a lesson to the rest of us."

There was a murmur of disbelief from Ronan, who exchanged a glance with his father, Daniel. The severity of the punishment was a sobering reminder of the stakes they all faced.

Rodrigo's face twisted with a mix of sorrow and frustration. "We sailed from Killybegs with nearly 1300 souls crammed onto that ship. The *Girona* moved slowly through the water, sluggish under the weight of so many. The smell—the stench of fear, sweat, and desperation—was unbearable. But we endured. We had no choice. We were running for our lives."

He took a deep breath, his voice growing heavier as he recounted the final, fateful night. "It was near midnight, October 26th, the third night of our journey north toward Scotland. That was when it hit. The worst storm I've ever seen. The sea seemed determined to keep us in Ireland, as if it had a claim on our souls. We tried—oh, we tried to row, to steer, to turn the sails—but the storm had us in its grip. Before we crashed, over a hundred men were lost, thrown overboard as the waves battered us relentlessly."

Rodrigo paused, his eyes distant, reliving the horror. "And then, without warning... a massive rock formation loomed ahead of us. There was no time to turn, no time to prepare. Almost everyone saw it at once, and we screamed—screamed for mercy, for Heaven's grace—but it wasn't to be. The *Girona* crashed violently against the rocks. The ship split apart like it was made of tinder."

The room was deathly silent, the crackling of the fire the only sound as Rodrigo's voice became a whisper. "Because I'd been thrown into the water on the *Duquesa Santa Ana,* I knew what to do. I didn't hesitate. I jumped. I found a piece of wood, a large timber, and I clung to it. While everyone else was trying to stay on the ship, I leaped into the waves, with only one thought in my mind—Marie. I had to survive for her."

He looked up, his eyes locking with Ronan's for a brief moment. "I rode the waves, crashing up and down. It carried me over a shallow range of rocks, away from the wreckage. I was pushed down the coast, nearly half a mile from where the ship broke apart. When I finally washed ashore... I looked back."

Rodrigo's voice trembled as he described the sight that haunted him. "It was chaos. Hundreds of bodies in the water, men clinging to the wreckage, only to be peeled away by the waves and smashed against the rocks. There was nothing I could do but watch. There was only a handful of survivors."

"How many?" Grace asked.

"Nine, including me."

"Nine!" Ronan said, bewildered. "What of Don Alonso? What of Vasquez?"

Rodrigo's eyes met Ronan's, the sorrow shared between them unspoken but clear. "They're gone, Ronan. The sea took them."

Ronan's chest tightened, a cold ache settling deep within him. The room seemed to blur as the weight of loss pressed against him. He glanced at Peggy, who sat quietly, her wide eyes shimmering with unshed tears. Turning back to Rodrigo, Ronan swallowed hard, his voice barely above a whisper. "I promised them, Rodrigo. I told Don Alonso I'd visit... I said I'd see Vasquez again. I was going to go."

Rodrigo reached out, his rough hand gripping Ronan's shoulder firmly. "I know, lad. And they knew it too. They spoke of ye with pride. You gave them hope when hope was scarce."

The knot in Ronan's chest loosened just a fraction, but the pain remained, raw and searing. He nodded slowly, eyes cast down. "Then I'll carry them with me, always. Their stories, their spirit. I won't let them be forgotten."

Peggy wiped a tear from her cheek, leaning into Ronan's side. The room stayed silent, the flicker of the hearth casting long shadows of loss and remembrance.

Grace, her face unreadable, finally broke the silence. "You survived for a reason, Rodrigo."

Rodrigo nodded, but the guilt and pain in his eyes remained. "Aye. For Marie. And for whatever comes next."

Ever After

Another wedding was held, this time with the full blessing of the entire village. The ceremony was simpler than the grand celebration Ronan had, but no less joyful. Marie, her eyes shining with happiness, stood by Rodrigo's side—now healed from his long ordeal. The villagers gathered around, their smiles warm, their hearts full of hope for the young couple who had endured so much.

After the vows were exchanged and the celebration quieted, Grace O'Malley called the couple aside. She stood tall, her striking presence commanding attention, her piercing eyes softened for this moment.

"Come here, both of ye," Grace said, her voice steady but carrying the weight of what she was about to offer. Marie and Rodrigo stepped forward, hands clasped tightly, their future shimmering before them.

"It will be too hard to live here," Grace began, her tone turning grave as she glanced toward the horizon. "Bingham is too close to Doona. His soldiers will always be a threat. You'll never find peace here."

Rodrigo's face tensed, his eyes flicking to Marie as his protective instinct stirred. He knew Grace spoke the truth. The looming danger from Bingham's men would haunt them if they stayed.

Grace continued, her gaze locking on Rodrigo's. "But you have done much for me, for my people, and for this land. I will grant you both a new life." She straightened, her voice now regal and firm. "I offer you land and a home by my castle at Rockfleet. You'll be safe there, under my protection."

Rodrigo's breath caught, a deep gratitude swelling inside him. This was more than he had dared to hope for. His fingers tightened around Marie's hand as he listened closely to the Pirate Queen.

"But one thing must change," Grace added, her eyes narrowing slightly as she studied Rodrigo. "You cannot keep the name Rodrigo. It will raise suspicion. From this day forward, you will be called Richard O'Malley. You will take my name and live under my banner."

Rodrigo—now Richard—looked at Grace with wide eyes, then turned to Marie. His heart swelled as he saw the brightness in her face, the hope for their future written in her gaze.

Grace shifted her focus to Marie, her voice softening. "And you, Marie, are now Marie O'Malley. You and your descendants will carry that name proudly. You will be under my protection for as long as I live—and beyond. Does that sit well with ye?"

Marie and Richard exchanged a long, meaningful glance. The weight of their journey, their survival, and their love all hung in that moment. Then, with wide smiles, they turned back to Grace, a quiet but powerful happiness filling their hearts.

"It does," Richard said, his voice firm but filled with gratitude. "It sits well with us both."

Marie nodded, her smile widening as her fingers intertwined with his. "More than well," she added, her voice catching with emotion. "We'll never have to worry again."

Grace grinned, her fierce expression softening as she looked upon the couple. "Then go," she said, her voice full of warmth. "Begin yer life in peace, and with the blessing of Heaven—and of me."

With those words, Richard and Marie O'Malley knew that their future was secure. They would start anew under the protection of the Pirate Queen, ready to build a life full of love and peace, far from the shadows of the past.

The End?

We think this is only the beginning.....

Rodrigo and Marie are Married at Grace's Castle

The Story of the Writing of Night of the Armada

Ever since I was nine years old and was brought over to Ireland for the first time by my dad, the idea of The Spanish Armada ships wrecking along the coast of Ireland during the great storm of 1588 has fascinated me. The idea inspired me to write the story, the Wancheen, a fictional historical Irish Thriller, which relies heavily on the Armada invasion in its plot.

But it is the ship that came aground in Doona, Ballycroy which most fascinates me. Why? Because it took place right along the shore where my ancestors land was, and because it was on that shore, when I was nine years old, that my cousin Danny Conway, only five at the time, told us there was treasure buried on the beach somewhere. He also told us that long ago, they could see part of the mast sticking up when the tide was out. Indeed, my dad, PJ, just told me last year, that his dad had found an old plank over twenty feet long buried in the sand one day at low tide, and that he had hung it in his barn for over twenty years.

Talk about peeking my curiosity.

Well, I decided the story needed to be told, in a more modern way, and that is what I tried to do. I hope you enjoyed it as much as I enjoyed writing it.

God Bless
D.P. Conway

Author's Note:

This book was developed with the help of artificial intelligence, specifically OpenAI's ChatGPT, which assisted in crafting the storyline, refining dialogue, and generating creative ideas. AI tools were also used in designing illustrations.

While all final decisions and edits were made by me, the AI played a significant role in shaping this unique collaboration between human creativity and technology.

See all D.P. Conway's books on Amazon
Search "**DP Conway Books**"

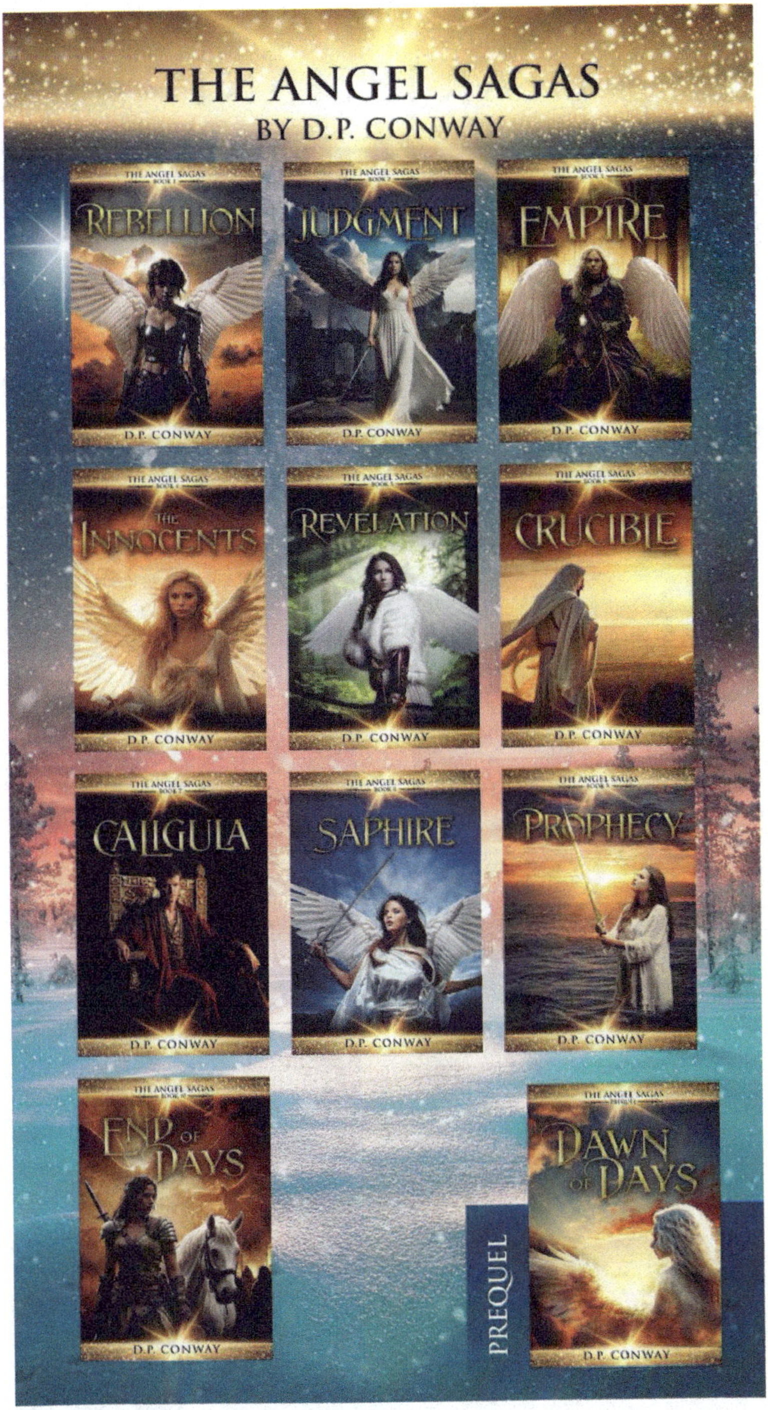
THE ANGEL SAGAS
BY D.P. CONWAY
REBELLION
JUDGMENT
EMPIRE
THE INNOCENTS
REVELATION
CRUCIBLE
CALLIGULA
SAPHIRE
PROPHECY
END OF DAYS
PREQUEL
DAWN OF DAYS
D.P. CONWAY

The Book "The Wancheen" is also set in Ireland

BEYOND THE VEIL
BY D.P. CONWAY
BEYOND THE VEIL
BOOKS
LAS VEGAS DOWN
The Story of the Route 91 Festival Shooting
D.P. CONWAY
BEYOND THE VEIL
BOOKS
PARKLAND
The Untold Story
D.P. CONWAY
BEYOND THE VEIL
BOOKS
THE WANCHEEN
A LONG HIDDEN MYSTERY OF OLD IRELAND
D.P. CONWAY
BEYOND THE VEIL
BOOKS
MARY
QUEEN OF HEARTS
D.P. CONWAY

Get the Latest on D.P. Conway's book releases.
Sign up at www.dpconway.com

D.P. Conway crafts stories that illuminate the human spirit and deepen our understanding of life's journey. Rooted in his Irish heritage and faith in life after death, he delves into the profound connection between this life and the Eternal World, pointing to our ultimate destiny in Heaven. His writings explore the timeless battle between darkness and light, affirming his conviction that goodness will prevail. Through his work, Conway inspires hope, resilience, and the courage to face life's challenges.

Copyright & Publication

Portions of the content in this book were created with the assistance of artificial intelligence, specifically OpenAI's ChatGPT. All intellectual property resulting from these contributions is owned and curated by the author.

Daylights Publishing
5498 Dorothy Drive Suite 3:16
Cleveland, OH 44070

www.dpconway.com
www.daylightspublishing.com

"Night of the Armada" is a work of fiction. All incidents, images, dialogue, and all characters, except for some well-known public figures, are products of the author's imagination and are not to be construed as real. Where real-life historical persons, images or places appear, the situations, incidents, and dialogues concerning those persons are entirely fictional and are not intended to depict actual events or to change the altogether fictional nature of the work. In all other respects, any resemblance to actual persons, living or deceased, events, institutions or locales is entirely coincidental.

Photo sources and credits are listed at www.dpconway.com

Cover: Nate Myers
Consultant: Laurence O'Bryan, Books Go Social, Dublin Ireland
Final Proof Reader: Marisa DiRuggiero Conway

Made in the USA
Columbia, SC
02 April 2025

56057217R00072